ABIE'S IRISH ROSE

ABIE'S IRISH ROSE

A Comedy in Three Acts

BY

ANNE NICHOLS

SAMUEL FRENCH

NEW YORK   LOS ANGELES

SAMUEL FRENCH LTD. LONDON

1937

MANUFACTURED IN THE UNITED STATES OF AMERICA
BY THE VAIL-BALLOU PRESS, INC., BINGHAMTON, N. Y.

"ABIE'S IRISH ROSE" was first produced by Miss Nichols at the Fulton Theatre in New York City. The play was directed by Laurence Marston and the cast was as follows:

MRS. ISAAC COHEN	*Mathilde Cottrelly*
ISAAC COHEN	*Bernard Gorcey*
DR. JACOB SAMUELS	*Howard Lang*
SOLOMON LEVY	*Alfred Wiseman*
ABRAHAM LEVY	*Robert B. Williams*
ROSE MARY MURPHY	*Marie Carroll*
PATRICK MURPHY	*John Cope*
FATHER WHALEN	*Harry Bradley*
FLOWER GIRL	*Dorothy Grau*

SYNOPSIS OF SCENES:

ACT ONE
Solomon Levy's Apartment, New York.

ACT TWO
Same as Act One. (One week later.)

ACT THREE
Abie and Rose Mary's Apartment, New York.
(Christmas Eve, one year later.)

ACT ONE

ACT ONE

SCENE: *The home of a New York business man, a prosperous one. The living room is comfortably furnished, without particular effort made to follow any special period, both as to architecture and decoration. The ensemble is rich in appearance and denotes very good taste.*

There are glass doors in the Right and Left walls, and two arches Right and Left Center in the back wall. There are glass double doors in these arches, opening off; the draperies on these doors cut off the view beyond when the doors are closed. In the Right Center hall is a stairway leading to the upper part of the house; and the main entrance is off Right. Beyond the Left Center arch is the conservatory. There is a window up Right.

At Right Center is a davenport with a library table behind it; a stand above the Right door and a table above the window; a hat tree in the hall together with a large lamp; a table and a chair up Center; a table and two chairs in the room up Left Center; a table up Left; a chair below Left door; a table and two chairs Left Center; a heavy chandelier hangs from the ceiling Center. The chandelier is

3

very ornate of the New York gas and electricity combined period.

In Act Two the room is decorated with orange trees in upper Right and Left corners. These are about eight feet high, with real oranges. There are smaller trees, poppies and other California flowers placed on the tables to give the room an atmosphere of California. Ribbons are attached to the chandelier and carried to the four corners of the room. The ribbons are orange in color with a small vine entwined around them, preferably bridal wreath or smilax.

The Left Center table has been removed and the chairs pushed aside. The Left Center doors are closed.

As the curtain goes up COHEN *is on the davenport. He has the funny part of the evening paper which he is reading with evident enjoyment.* MRS. COHEN *and* RABBI *are seated at table Left Center.* MRS. COHEN *in chair Right and* RABBI *in chair Left.*

At rise COHEN *laughs.* MRS. COHEN *gives him a look and continues speech.*

MRS. COHEN. Yes sir, I says to Isaac, says I, "Isaac call the doctor, I know ven I god a differend pain. Ven my indegestive tablets don't voik, I know how I veel!" [COHEN *laughing uproariously at the funny paper. The* RABBI *looks at him.* MRS. COHEN *is furious at this interruption. Continues with her monologue.*] So Isaac he calls the doctor. [COHEN *laughs again, which inter-*

ACT I

See page 3

rupts MRS. COHEN. *She looks at him, then at the* RABBI.] Such a foolishness! [*She gives* COHEN *another look which he doesn't see, so interested in his paper is he, then she turns back again to the* RABBI.] Vhere was I?

RABBI. [*Impatiently.*] Isaac had just called the doctor.

MRS. COHEN. Oh, yess! Und de doctor came und:— [COHEN *laughs again.* MRS. COHEN *stops, looks at* COHEN *furiously.* COHEN *takes paper down from his face.*] Will you stop dot laughing at nodings! [*Crosses to* COHEN.]

COHEN. [*Laughs to himself, vaguely hearing her, then it penetrates that he has been spoken to. There is a deep silence. He looks up.* MRS. COHEN *is looking daggers at him. The* RABBI *is trying not to laugh.*] Huh? Vot? You speak to me, Mama?

MRS. COHEN. Such a foolishness! Laughing at nodings!

COHEN. [*Hurt.*] Mama. I was laughing at Maggy and Jiggs. Such a vife!

MRS. COHEN. [*Sore now and ready for an argument.*] Oh, so you voss laughing at the vife?

COHEN. No. No, I'm keeping up with Maggy and Jiggs. [*He picks up the paper again. His face beams as he starts to read. Reading—* "What a man— What a man, just like me." MRS. COHEN *sits at the table.*] Mama, listen. "You big walrus why don'd you go into some pizzness, instead of loafing all day; ged oud of my sight." Dod's Maggy vot she says. Und Jiggs he says, vid de cigar in his mout and his hands on his hips, "Vell," says Jiggs, "Maggy" dods the wife from Jiggs.

"Vell," says Jiggs, "Maggy, you soitantly kin tink of disagreeable tings." [COHEN *laughs. The* RABBI *is also interested.*]

MRS. COHEN. [*Rises, with her face all set for a fight. Her mouth gathered together into a little knot.*] Is dod funny?

COHEN. Vait a minute! [*Laughs.*] Und Jiggs goes oud for a pizzness!

RABBI. Is that the one, Isaac, where he goes into business with Mr. Duem?

COHEN. [*Laughing uproariously.*] Yess, und meets all the pretty girls. [*Crossing to* MRS. COHEN; *shows her paper and nudges her.*] Und Maggy catches him making lofe to the stenographer. [*Laughing, crosses back to davenport; sits.*] Ain't that funny, Mama?

MRS. COHEN. [*Now thoroughly disgusted with both of them.*] I'm dying with laughing! [RABBI *laughing at the thought of it.* MRS. COHEN *sits.* COHEN *looks at her; stops laughing, then picks up his paper, turns it over and looks at another page.* MRS. COHEN *looks at him satisfied she will not be interrupted again. The* RABBI *yawns behind his hand.*] Vot vass I talking aboud?

RABBI. Your operation!

MRS. COHEN. Oh, yes. Where vas I—in the hospital?

RABBI. Oh, no. Isaac had just called the doctor.

MRS. COHEN. Und the doctor he came. Und I said— "good evening, Doctor." Und the doctor he say "good evening"—and—

RABBI. And did he diagnose the case as appendicitis?

MRS. COHEN. Like that. Didn't he, Isaac? [*There is a pause, then* COHEN *looks up.*]

COHEN. Oh yes, sure, Mama. [*He turns back—then.*]

RABBI. And did he operate immediately?

MRS. COHEN. No, he didn't want to.

RABBI. Didn't want to?

MRS. COHEN. He didn't want to. Did he, Isaac? [*Pause.*] *Did he Isaac?!!!!?*

COHEN. No.—No. [*Pause.*] Didn't want to what, Mama?

MRS. COHEN. Didn't want to operate.

COHEN. Oh, the doctor. No. [*He turns back again to paper.*]

RABBI. I sympathize with you, Mrs. Cohen.

MRS. COHEN. I tell you, Doctor Samuels, it is the woman what silently suffers.

COHEN. Yes, Mama—you were silent with the ether, but you haven't been silent ever since.

MRS. COHEN. Oh, I don't talk so much.

COHEN. Yes, you do, Mama. Always you talk about ether.

MRS. COHEN. I didn't say a word about the ether.

COHEN. But, Mama—

MRS. COHEN. Ssh—Isaac!!!

COHEN. All right, noo—

RABBI. I wonder what is keeping our good host.

MRS. COHEN. He went to find Sarah—someone called him on the phone, and Sarah couldn't hear the message. He's waiting for it to ring any minute. Poor Solomon.

COHEN. See. Why do you say "poor Solomon," Mama? He ain't poor.

MRS. COHEN. Papa—always you—argue—

COHEN. But, Mama. Poor is arem and arem is poor. If he ain't arem how can he be poor—

MRS. COHEN. But why should you always argue— *Shweig Shtill!*

RABBI. You know—we three might help Solomon—

MRS. COHEN. How?

RABBI. Have you ever tried concentration?

COHEN. Concentration?

RABBI. I mean, keep quiet—not talk.

COHEN. Mama did vonce, but it didn't agree vid her.

RABBI. I mean to concentrate, to think!

MRS. COHEN. All I can think of vos dod operation.

RABBI. If we three concentrate, think, all together, that we want that telephone to ring again and relieve Solomon's mind about Abie it might result successfully.

COHEN. If it does, I'll concentrate on a million dollars.

MRS. COHEN. Let's try. It don't cost nothink!

RABBI. Very well! Now for one minute think hard that you want *that telephone to ring.*
[*All sit thinking. Fifteen seconds pass; the clock strikes one,* ALL *sit up nervously.* COHEN *assumes a pose of "The Thinker."* MRS. COHEN *looks at the time.*]

MRS. COHEN. How early it iss of late!

RABBI. Ssh! Concentrate, *my friends! Concentrate!*

[COHEN *repeats "Thinker" pose.* ALL *sit again quietly. The doorbell rings violently.* SOLOMON *enters from door Left.*]

SOLOMON. Vos dod the phone? [*Sees the* RABBI.]

MRS. COHEN. No. Mr. Levy, dot vas the doorbell.

SOLOMON. [*To* MRS. COHEN.] Thank you. Hello, Doctor Samuels; glad to see you! Eggscuse me blease! Sarah can't hear a void over the phone and she can'd hear the doorpell any more—keeps me busy running my servants errands. [*Doorbell rings again.*] Hello, Isaac. [*Said as he goes to door. He exits quickly out Right Center.*]

MRS. COHEN. Why he don't discharge Sarah is more than I could learn.

COHEN. Poor Solomon! He's worried about Abie. [*This is to the* RABBI.] He vosn't to the store all day!

MRS. COHEN. Sowin' his vild oats!

RABBI. Nonsense. I know his son Abie as well as I know his father, and if Abie has been away from the store all day, he has had a very good reason, you'll see.

MRS. COHEN. Dod's *vod you say!* [*She squints her eye knowingly. The telephone rings,* SOLOMON *rushes in like mad. Answers telephone on table Right Center.*] Yess, dod vos the phone dod time, Solomon. [*She says this in a most sympathetic manner as much as to say "poor thing, I pity you."*]

SOLOMON. [*Grabs the telephone, picking it up.*] Thank God! [*He has the receiver off the hook by this time.*] Hello! Who iss it? Yes vot? Me! Yes, it's me! Who am me? Say who am you? What number? I don't know the number! I didn't get the phone to call myself! Oh, Abie wishes to speak vid his fadder? Pud him on! [*To* RABBI.] Abie. [SOLOMON *laughs at* OTHERS. MRS. COHEN *makes a knowing face at* COHEN, *they are* ALL *interested.* SOLOMON *seems very angry at the telephone.*] Hello! Iss dod you? Oh it iss? Vell you—you—loafer! V-here have you been all tay and vot iss it? I've a good notion to— Vot? Huh? A vod vid you? You vont to bring a lady home to dinner? [*He turns to* COHEN *and winks, belying his bad humor. In a whisper, as though* ABIE *could hear.*] He vonts to bring a lady home to dinner! [*Then back in the telephone again.*]

COHEN. [*To* SOLOMON, *who with his eyes warns* COHEN *of* MRS. COHEN'S *presence.*] Oy, I can't wait! [*Throws one leg excitedly over the other. Turns around, sees* MRS. COHEN—*and is squelched.*]

SOLOMON. Vot, I didn't heard you—say it twice! Oh,

she's a very sweet girl? Oh I vill, vill I? [*He turns to
them again.*] He says I'll like her! She's a sveet girl.
[*Then immediately back into telephone.*] Jewish? [*He
smiles and turns to them again.*] He says, vait till I
see her! [*Then back in the telephone again.*] You little
goniff—I smell a mices! Sure! I'll tell Sarah. Goodbye,
Abie, goodbye. [*He hangs up receiver. They* ALL *sit
waiting for him to tell them everything.*] Ha, ha,
peoples, my Abie's got a girl. Maybe the good Rabbi
will soon officiate at a wedding. Eh? [*Crosses to Center. He is delighted.*]

COHEN. Is she Hebrew?

SOLOMON. Of course. Hebrew. Jewish Hebrew. [*He
is delighted. He nudges* COHEN.] Abie! says, vait till
I see her! [*Turns to* RABBI.] Doctor Samuels—"Lieber
Freund"— Maybe we'll all be goin' to a vedding soon!
Yes! [*Crosses to back of table Left Center.*]

COHEN. Solomon, why are you trying to get Abie
married? He's happy.

MRS. COHEN. You mean to say he wouldn't be happy if
he was married?

COHEN. Mama, can't I talk at all?

RABBI. Oh, Isaac didn't mean to infer he isn't happy.
He is happy, aren't you, Isaac?

COHEN. Perfectly.

SOLOMON. No, it isn't the idea that I want my Abie
married exactly, but I want his grandchildren. [*Crosses
Center.*]

COHEN. You don't want him to get married. But you want him to have children. Mama listen to that.

MRS. COHEN. Isaac, you don't know what Solomon means.

COHEN. Sure, I do, he—

MRS. COHEN. You don't understand a word he says—

COHEN. Concentrate, Mama, concentrate.

SOLOMON. Yes, Isaac, I want grandchildren—dozens of them. [*Crosses to* COHEN.]

COHEN. Right away you talk wholesale.

SOLOMON. You see before my Abie was born, Rebecca and I we always used to plan for him. I wanted him to be a politician. Rebecca says, "no, Solomon. I want my boy—our son—to stay close by his father."

COHEN. And he certainly has.

SOLOMON. Yes.

RABBI. Yes, I don't know what your business would have done without him.

SOLOMON. Neither do I. But don't you tell him I said so.

MRS. COHEN. Why don't you take him into the firm?

RABBI. Right. Solomon Levy and Son—that wouldn't sound bad at all.

SOLOMON. *That's* just exactly what I am going to do. When he's married—not before.

RABBI. Why must you wait until he's married?

SOLOMON. Did you ever see any of Abie's girls?

RABBI. No.

SOLOMON. Not one Jewish and my Abie is not going to marry anyone but a Jewish girl if I can help it.

COHEN. Maybe you won't be able to help it.

SOLOMON. Who said it, not be able to help it? Let him try and you'll see how I could help it.

MRS. COHEN. Are you sure that this new girl is the right one?

SOLOMON. Didn't he say wait till I see her? Oh, what a relief when I'll see that son of mine safely married. I must tell Sarah dinner for three— [*Crosses to door Left.*]

MRS. COHEN. [*Rises and starts to go.*] Ve must be going.

SOLOMON. Den please come back later and take a look at her.

MRS. COHEN. If ve can, ve vill.

COHEN. Vhy can't we, Mama? [*Rises, crosses to Center.*]

MRS. COHEN. [*To* COHEN.] Because I'm awfully tired and you ought to go to bed early.

COHEN. [*Crestfallen; To door Right Center.*] See— she's tired, and I got to go to bed early. [*Going out through hall followed by* MRS. COHEN.]

RABBI. [*Starting for the door. Right Center.*] I'll drop in later, Solomon.

SOLOMON. Goodbye, peoples, goodbye, and don't forget. When my Abie says a thing you can build a bank on it. [*Going to arch Right Center. To photograph on table up Center.*] Abele, Boyele meiner.

[SOLOMON *takes out cigarette paper, puts in two pinches of tobacco, singing "Masseltof" as he reaches Left Center door, moistens cigarette, causes discord, in song and exits Left Center.* ABIE *enters the room from Right Center cautiously looking about, then he beckons to* ROSE MARY *who enters after him. They are both nervous and frightened.* ABIE *looks upstairs, listens a moment, then comes down to door Left, opens it, listens, then closes it carefully, not making any noise. He goes to door Right and repeats business, then back to arch Right Center.*]

ABIE. Well, the coast is clear. [*Crosses to* ROSE MARY, *Center.*]

ROSE MARY. [*Coming down to Abie.*] Oh, Abie, I'm so frightened!

ABIE. With a perfectly good husband to protect you?

ROSE MARY. Oh, I forgot!

ABIE. [*Takes her in his arms.*] You haven't been married long enough yet to be used to it. Let's see— [*Looks at his watch.*] Just one hour and thirty-three minutes. Do you realize, young lady, you are no longer Rose Mary Murphy? You are Mrs. Abraham Levy.

ROSE MARY. Mrs. Abraham Levy! Glory be to God!

ABIE. Isn't it wonderful?

ROSE MARY. Abie, we will both be disowned.

ABIE. Well, that's better than being separated for the rest of our lives, isn't it?

ROSE MARY. [*Hesitating over it.*] Yes.

ABIE. Why do you say it that way?

ROSE MARY. I am not so sure that they won't try to separate us.

ABIE. Oh, yes, try. But we're not going to let them. Are we?

ROSE MARY. No.

ABIE. [*Takes her in his arms.*] We were married good and tight by a nice Methodist minister.

ROSE MARY. "Till death do us part."

ABIE. [*Breaks embrace and takes her hands.*] Oh, that reminds me, why did you refuse to say "I do" to the obey me?

ROSE MARY. [*With a slight brogue, smiling.*] Shure—I'm that Irish!

ABIE. I didn't balk when he said "repeat after me, With all my worldly goods I thee endow." You know it's fifty-fifty.

ROSE MARY. To be sure it is. Faith you haven't any worldly goods and your father is liable to disown you when he finds out you haven't married a nice little Jewish girl.

ABIE. So is your father, when he finds out you haven't married a nice little Irish boy.

ROSE MARY. [*With true Irish foresight.*] That would be fifty-fifty. [*Backs to front of davenport.*]

ABIE. You know, Rose Mary, I was just thinking. [*Crosses down Left of davenport.*]

ROSE MARY. You are liable to have to do a whole lot of thinking, so you had better get into practice. [*Sits on davenport. He sits with her.*]

ABIE. No, in all seriousness, Rose Mary, you know I'm sure Father will be crazy about you.

ROSE MARY. [*Lapsing into brogue.*] He might be crazy about me all right, but when he hears about "me religion" he'll be crazier.

ABIE. Silly, isn't it, to be so narrow-minded. Well, he can't any more than tell us to go, can he?

ROSE MARY. But Abie—you work for your father!

ABIE. Yep! [*Sighing.*] And if you don't make a hit with him, I'm liable to lose my job. I should worry. I'll find another.

ROSE MARY. And if you lost your job I'll have to do my own housework, and learn to cook.

ABIE. You can fry eggs, can't you?

ROSE MARY. I can, but I can't turn them over.

ABIE. [*With his arm around her.*] I'll turn them over for you. [*She cuddles close to him, forgetting for an instant what is coming.*]

ROSE MARY. Oh, Abie! Will you always be willing to do so much for me?

ABIE. Always! [ABIE *and* ROSE MARY *sigh.*]

ROSE MARY. Abie!

ABIE. [*Holding her close.*] Yes, dear?

ROSE MARY. Wouldn't it be wonderful if our fathers would take our marriage nicely!

ABIE. [*Hugging her closer.*] Wonderful!

ROSE MARY. Then we wouldn't have to worry about a thing. You could go on with your job—and—

ABIE. Now, you stop worrying about that, dear. I'm sure Father will fall in love with you as I did, on first sight.

ROSE MARY. Abie, you're a dear! You know sometimes [*Lapsing into brogue.*] I think you've a bit of the Irish tucked away in you somewhere. Faith, I believe you're half Irish.

ABIE. [*Right back at her with a brogue.*] To be sure Mavourneen, my better half is Irish.

ROSE MARY. [*Laughing.*] And my better half is Jewish. [*Puts right hand on his cheek.*]

ABIE. What could be sweeter? [*Kiss. In embrace.* SOLOMON *sings off Left.*] That's Father!

ROSE MARY. [*Frightened. Both rise.*] Oh, Abie!

ABIE. Don't weaken, dear! And no matter what he says, remember he's a peach when you get under his skin.

ROSE MARY. I hope it isn't a long way under.

[ABIE *crosses to Center.* ROSE MARY *behind him walking lockstep. Hides behind* ABIE *on* SOLOMON'S *entrance.*

SOLOMON *enters; front of table Left Center to Center. He is a good natured man with a round Jewish face. Hard work has made him older than his years, but hard luck has only softened his nature. He is a prosperous business man now, but still wears the comfortable old clothes of his other years. He is not stingy, but having known the want of things in days gone by he wastes nothing extravagantly. He sees* ABIE—*does not notice* ROSE MARY *who is standing back of* ABIE—SOLOMON *singing "Oi— Oi—"*]

ABIE. [*Trying to be casual.*] Hello, Dad.

SOLOMON. Vell? [*Hands behind him. Stopping short.*] You loafer! Vhere hafe you peen all afternoon?

ABIE. Away. [*Crosses to* SOLOMON. ROSE MARY *follows close behind, unseen by* SOLOMON.]

SOLOMON. Is dod an excuse— Away?

ABIE. Certainly not, but—

SOLOMON. [*Not letting him get in a word edgeways.*] Und de pizzness! Pi! Such a day! Vid everybody esking for you.

ABIE. Missed me, eh, Dad?

SOLOMON. [*Angrily.*] Loafer! [*Turns to Left. On word "Loafer"* ROSE MARY *quickly goes to arch Right Center and watches the two from behind draperies.* ABIE *tries to find* ROSE MARY *with hands behind him.*] Nobody vants me to vait on dem. It's "vhere is Abraham, Mr. Levy? Vhere your son iss, Mr. Levy? No tank you, Mr. Levy. I'll vait for your son, Mr. Levy, he knows eggsactly vot I vant, Mr. Levy." All tay long! Abie I'm not going to stand for this nonsense—

ABIE. [*With a winning smile.*] Now, Dad—

SOLOMON. [*Holds* ABIE *off, and looks at him fondly, then he hugs him to him.*] Abie—Boyele meiner—

[ROSE MARY *enters laughing; comes down Center.* SOLOMON *sees* ROSE MARY, *who has been standing watching this scene intently. He looks at her first as if he cannot believe his eyes—drops* ABIE *and steps back. Her smile fades.*]

ABIE. Dad—this—is—the lady I just phoned you about. [*Looking at* ROSE MARY—*then back again at his father. Taking* ROSE MARY *by the hand and leading her to his father.*] Dad, I want you to meet a very dear friend of mine!

SOLOMON. [*Looks at* ROSE MARY *skeptically.*] Who's de name blease?

ABIE. [*Ignoring the question.*] I met her just before the Armistice was signed!

SOLOMON. [*Not at all friendly.*] Iss dod so?

ROSE MARY. Yes, in France!!

[ABIE *and* ROSE MARY *do not know what to say.*]

SOLOMON. A trained nurse, dod's a pizzness!

ROSE MARY. Well, I wasn't exactly a trained nurse.

SOLOMON. [*Looking at her skeptically.*] No? Well, I had a trained nurse vonce and she wasn't eggsactly von either.

ABIE. [*Trying to break the tenseness of the situation.*] She was an entertainer, Dad. You know, keeping the boys' minds off the war. Making it easier for them, you know!

SOLOMON. Yes, I know. [*Looking at* ROSE MARY'S *prettiness and believing it.*]

ROSE MARY. I used to sing for the boys in back of the lines.

SOLOMON. Oy—an actress!

ROSE MARY. Mercy, no!

ABIE. [*Impatiently.*] Dad!

SOLOMON. Vell, you introduced me *vonce* to an actress. And believe me *dod* girl could act. Her name was O'Brien! Oi! Vod a name! [ABIE *backs up a step.* ABIE *and* ROSE MARY *exchange glances.* ROSE MARY *crosses to front of davenport.*] I tought you vos an actress, too, by the dress.

ROSE MARY. [*Trying to laugh.*] You think this dress is loud?

SOLOMON. It's not so quiet—und there ain'd much of id. [*He motions with his hands that the dress is short.*] Maybe it shrunk!

ABIE. [*Coming down Center.*] Of course, it didn't shrink. All the girls are wearing their dresses short this year, Dad.

SOLOMON. Iss dod so? Well, boy, your mudder always wore long dresses. [*Looking skeptically at* ROSE MARY'S *legs.*]

ABIE. I'll bet if Mother were alive today she would be wearing short dresses too. [*Crosses up.*]

ROSE MARY. [*Steps toward him.*] It's much more sanitary, Mr. Levy. Long skirts trailing along the ground get full of microbes.

SOLOMON. The microbes would have some high jump to make dod hem.

[*She turns away.*]

ABIE. [*Who is dreadfully ill at ease.*] Never mind, Rose. [*Crosses to Left of davenport.*]

SOLOMON. [*Suspiciously.*] Rose? Rose vot?

ROSE MARY. Rose Mary.

SOLOMON. [*Closing up like a clam toward her.*] Dot's vot I thought.

ABIE. You thought what! [*Crosses Center to* SOLOMON.]

SOLOMON. Ven my son goes vid a girl, dot girl must speak the English language like a Jewess.

ABIE. [*Goes up a step.*] Father!

SOLOMON. [*Sternly.*] Still!!! [*Crossing to* ROSE MARY. ABIE *drops his head and goes up.*] I have nodings against you. I like Rose. I like the name of Rose. *Mary* might have been a grand old name, but I don't like it.

ROSE MARY. My name was good enough for my mother, sure it's good enough for me.

ABIE. [*Comes down Left of* SOLOMON.] Of course it is!

SOLOMON. Vell, tell me, vhere did you learn does Irish expressions? Sure!

ROSE MARY. [*Very proudly.*] From my father.

SOLOMON. [*Now highly suspicious.*] Hah! Iss dod so?

ABIE. [*Interrupting hastily.*] Why yes, Dad. He was once an actor.

SOLOMON. *So?* Vell vot is *his* name? Is it Mary too?

ROSE MARY. My father's name Mary?

SOLOMON. You just said your name vos Rose *Mary.*

ABIE. [*Interrupting hastily again.*] His name is Solomon!

SOLOMON. Oh! Your name is Rose Mary Solomon?

ROSE MARY. [*Very indignant.*] Certainly not!

SOLOMON. [*Quickly.*] Oh, your father's *first* name is Solomon?

ABIE. [*Quickly.*] Yes! [ROSE MARY *looks at him—he is too fast for her—she gasps, so quickly has* ABIE *retorted.*]

SOLOMON. Oh! Well, Solomon vhot? [*Turns to* ROSE MARY.]

ROSE MARY. Murphy— [SOLOMON *looks at her quickly;* ABIE *interrupts and finishes before* ROSE MARY *knows exactly what he is doing.*]

ABIE. [*Quickly.*] Miss Murpheski.

SOLOMON. Murpheski! say dod's a fine nize name!

Now there you are. [ROSE MARY *is so taken back by this interruption of* ABIE'S *she is speechless.*] At first I tought you vouldn't have a name like dod. You don'd look id!

ABIE. No, she doesn't, does she?

SOLOMON. [*Looking at* ROSE MARY.] Faces are very deceiving! [*Smiling benignly for the first time on* ROSE MARY.] Take off your coad, Miss Murpheski! [*He turns to* ABIE *very reprovingly.*] Abie, I'm surprised at your inhospitality! Honest! [*He turns back to* ROSE MARY, *takes her wrap, looks at the material very closely, putting his glass on to do so.*] You buy fine materials, Miss Murpheski.

ROSE MARY. Thank you.

SOLOMON. Noo, Abe, voss shtaistie vie a laimener goilem. Hang it up. [*Gives coat to* ABIE. ABIE *takes coat to hall, hangs it up and returns to rear of davenport.*] Sit down, Miss Murpheski. Ay, ay, ay! [*Sitting on davenport.*] Dod's some ring you are varing, yes? [*Breathes on ring.* ABIE *standing behind davenport makes motions over* SOLOMON'S *shoulder to* ROSE MARY.]

ROSE MARY. Yes, my father gave me that.

SOLOMON. Oh, your papa! [*After* ROSE MARY *has seated herself at Right of table he settles himself back contentedly for a chat.*] So you and Abie have known each odder a long time, eh?

ROSE MARY. Oh, yes. We met in France! Your son's a wonderful hero, Mr. Levy, do you realize that?

SOLOMON. Ain'd he my son? How could he be anything else? [ABIE *comes down.* SOLOMON *smiles on him proudly.*]

ABIE. With such a father, eh! Dad? [ABIE *is kidding, but* SOLOMON *hasn't that kind of a sense of humor.* ABIE *comes down to Left Center.*]

SOLOMON. Dod's vhat I *say!*—You know every time dot— [*He turns to* ROSE MARY, *rising, offering his hand.*] Oi! I'm pleased to meet you, Miss Murpheski!

[*This comes as a surprise to* ROSE MARY. SOLOMON *goes to* ABIE.]

ROSE MARY. Thank you.

SOLOMON. Abie, ve must esk Miss Murpheski to stay to supper, yes?

ABIE. I phoned you that she would stay to dinner.

SOLOMON. [*Crosses to Left Center.*] Oh, yes, dod's so.

ROSE MARY. I don't want to be any trouble.

SOLOMON. *Nod* at all! Miss Murpheski. Eggscuse me, I'll speak to Sarah. Murpheski! Abele boyele meiner! Murpheski!

[*He exits Left, leaving* ROSE MARY *and* ABIE *together.* ROSE MARY *turns to* ABIE *furiously.*]

ROSE MARY. [*Rises.*] Murpheski!

ABIE. Rose Mary, I just had to do it. I saw that he wasn't even going to give himself a chance to like you.

ROSE MARY. I don't want him to like me! Murpheski! [*Hides her face.*] Oh, Shades of St. Patrick!

ABIE. [*Trying to calm her.*] Rose Mary, dear—

ROSE MARY. He even objects to my first name. First thing I know you'll be calling me Rebecca!

ABIE. Sssh! He'll hear you. [*Looking off Left.*]

ROSE MARY. I want him to hear me. I was never so insulted in my life. Sure, Murphy's a grand name— I don't know why you had to tack "ski" on to it. [*Crying.*]

ABIE. I know, dear, but if I had told him your name was Murphy we wouldn't have had a chance. It's our happiness *I'm* fighting for!

ROSE MARY. But he'll have to know some day that I'm Irish!

ABIE. I have a grand idea.

ROSE MARY. If it's anything like the last few you've sprung on me, please don't tell me. [*Crosses and sits on davenport.*]

ABIE. [*Slight pause—then crosses to her. Sits beside her.*] Listen! You love me, don't you? [*Pause.*]

ROSE MARY. Ah, Abie darling, that's the trouble, I do love you.

ABIE. [*Sits—embraces her—slight pause.*] And you want our married life to be a happy one, don't you?

ROSE MARY. It's going to be, I can see that much from here.

ABIE. Then listen, dear, let him think your name is Murpheski. Make him like Miss Murpheski, then maybe Miss

Murpheski can persuade him to open his heart a little bit to Miss Murphy. See what I mean?

ROSE MARY. You mean, I'm to let him think I'm Jewish until he likes me?

ABIE. Yes.

ROSE MARY. If he learns to like me, you think he might sanction our marriage?

ABIE. I'm sure of it. You know when you married me this morning you took me for better or for worse.

ROSE MARY. This is the worst I ever heard of.

ABIE. I'd do as much for you. You know your father isn't going to be easy either.

ROSE MARY. Don't remind me of my father at this minute. Your father is enough trouble for one day.

ABIE. That's what I say, dear, let's win my father over to our side, then when your father comes on from California, we'll have my father to help win your father.

ROSE MARY. You don't know my *father*— [*They kiss.*]

SOLOMON. [*Enter* SOLOMON *to front of table Left Center.*] Vell, dod's dod! [*Smiling again upon them, they stop kissing—look a bit uneasy and separate as they turn to him.*] Go right ahead, don't let me inderrupt!

ABIE. [*Rising.*] Oh, Dad, come over here—I want you to know Miss Murpheski better. [*Brings him to davenport.*]

SOLOMON. [*Sits on davenport.*] Vell, dod's fair enough!

I am glad of vone thing totay! [BOTH *look at* SOLOMON *expectantly.*] Dod you ain't an actress—!

ROSE MARY. Then I'm glad I'm not too!

SOLOMON. What do you do for a living?

ROSE MARY. [*The question has been fired so quickly at her she is stunned.*] Nothing.

SOLOMON. *Dod's* a great way to live. I don't believe in it.

ROSE MARY. My father never would let me work. I must study.

SOLOMON. [*Smiling again.*] Your father he has money!

[*All this time,* ABIE *is fidgeting about, embarrassed.*]

ABIE. He's in business on the Coast.

SOLOMON. Vat business, Abie? Cloiding?

ROSE MARY. No, contracting!

SOLOMON. [*Immediately freezing again.*] Murpheski— contracting?

ABIE. Contracting for clothes.

SOLOMON. What!

ROSE MARY. [*Getting* ABIE's *meaning quickly.*] Yes, con- tracting for clothes.

SOLOMON. Contracting for— Oh yes, yes I know. I know. I must—look him up. [*Pleased at this—takes out note- book, writes.*] Look him up. You know a lod aboud her father's business, Abie. [*Jokingly.*]

ABIE. Why, I know what Miss Murpheski has told me.

SOLOMON. Vell the cloiding is a good pizzness. [ABIE *and* ROSE MARY *exchange glances,* BOTH *are nervous and trying to make a hit.*] Abie!

ABIE. Yes, Dad?

SOLOMON. Vhy didn't you speak before of Miss Murpheski to me?

ABIE. Oh, I don't know.

SOLOMON. [*Nudges* ROSE MARY.] I hate to tell you, Miss Murpheski, never before has Abie had such a nice little Jewish girl.

ROSE MARY. [*Trying to laugh.*] Is that so?

SOLOMON. You tell 'em! But, Rose Mary—that's a fine name for a Jewish girl. Rose Mary!

ABIE. Why don't you tell Dad how you got the Mary part of it.

SOLOMON. [*Turning to* ROSE MARY.] Vod does he mean got the Mary's?

ROSE MARY. [*Not knowing what* ABIE *is thinking of saying.*] Why you see, Mr. Levy— You tell him, Abie.

ABIE. [*Short embarrassed pause.*] Well, you see, Dad, her name is really Rosie!

SOLOMON. [*Smiling broadly.*] Rosie! Vell, I thought so!

ABIE. Rosie Murpheski!

SOLOMON. Yeh, but the Mary's?

ROSE MARY. [*Coming to* ABIE'S *rescue, who is hardly able to come up for air.*] Well, I thought Mary was such a pretty name, so I took it.

SOLOMON. Give it back! Rosie is a peautiful name. You don't need the rest of it. [ABIE *sits on Right arm of davenport.*]

ROSE MARY. All right, if you say so.

SOLOMON. [*This flatters him.*] You hear dod, Abie? If I say so! Oh, Abele— [*Laughs.*] I never knew you had such a good taste. [*Looking at* ROSE MARY *and pinching her cheek.*] And Abie—has known you ever since the Var?

ROSE MARY. Yes—but you see I live in California. I went home as soon as I came back from France.

SOLOMON. Are you visiting somebody here now?

ROSE MARY. No, I'm staying at the Pennsylvania.

SOLOMON. In the depot?

ABIE. Dad! The Pennsylvania Hotel!!!!

SOLOMON. Oi, such an expense! Abie right away quick you should get Rosie's trunk away from dod place.

ROSE MARY. But Mr. Levy!

SOLOMON. Tut—tut—tut! *This* is your New York home. I like you, Rosie. I vouldn't have you staying in such a hotel.

ABIE. But Dad, maybe Miss Murpheski prefers to stay in a hotel.

SOLOMON. Nonsense! Rosie stays here, where she can get some nice Kosher food. [*Turns to* ROSIE.] You like dod?

ROSE MARY. [*Isn't able to say anything to it.*] I love it.

SOLOMON. [*To* ABIE.] See, she loves it. I vouldn't think of letting her go avay from here. [*He turns to* ROSE MARY, *smiles—she smiles back—*ABIE *is frantic—but can say nothing.*] Abie, run over to the Cohen's, and ask Mrs. Cohen if Mr. Cohen can come over. I want him to meet Rosie.

ABIE. Why not ask Mrs. Cohen too. She's a peach, Miss Murpheski—you'd like her.

SOLOMON. [*Skeptically.*] Yes. Esk *her* too. She hasn't any appendix, but she's a nice woman.

ROSE MARY. Oh, I see—she's just been operated on?

SOLOMON. Yes. About three or four years ago. She'll tell you about it.

ABIE. You might as well hear it tonight and get it over with. She tells everybody.

ROSE MARY. I love to hear of operations.

SOLOMON. Then run along, Abie. And, Abie—

ABIE. [*Up to arch Right Center.*] Yes, Dad.

SOLOMON. Don't hurry back. Joke. Yes. [*Crosses up to arch Right Center. He laughs at his own jokes all the time.*]

ABIE. [*Laughs.*] Dad, shall I ask the Cohens to stay for dinner?

SOLOMON. For vhat? We're not celebrating anything. A business for giving dinners for nothing. [ABIE *exits, going Right through hall, smiling.* SOLOMON *turns to* ROSE MARY. *Pause.*] I don't know how Abie ever kept you a secred so long.

ROSE MARY. Well, we were afraid, you wouldn't like me.

SOLOMON. Ain't dod foolishness? [*Comes down to her.*]

ROSE MARY. Abie wanted to tell you about me.

SOLOMON. Abie is it? [*Nudging her jokingly.*]

ROSE MARY. Hearing you call him Abie—it came natural to me.

SOLOMON. That's right. Keep it up! I like to hear you call him Abie! He's a vonderful boy, my Abie!

ROSE MARY. Indeed he is!

SOLOMON. You like him?

ROSE MARY. Very much; he's a splendid man.

SOLOMON. You don't know the half of it. All by myself I raised him.

ROSE MARY. [*Softly.*] Yes, I know. Abie told me his mother died when he was born. [SOLOMON *nods his head,* "*yes.*"] My mother died when I was born, too.

SOLOMON. [*Turning to her.*] Your father raised you, too? [ROSE MARY *nods her head.* SOLOMON *throws up his hands.*] I can sympathize with him.

[*At this* ROSE MARY *is taken back.*]

ROSE MARY. My father is a wonderful man!

SOLOMON. Of course he is, isn't his name Murpheski!
[*Turns away.*] What did Abie say his first name was?

ROSE MARY. [*Thinking quickly.*] Why—Solomon!

SOLOMON. Solomon Murpheski! [ROSE MARY *quickly
crosses herself.*] I'd like to shake the hand of Solomon
Murpheski.

ROSE MARY. [*With double meaning.*] I wish you could.
[*Laughing.*]

[MRS. COHEN *enters Right Center. She is a tall good-
looking woman, very well dressed.*]

MRS. COHEN. Hello, Mr. Levy. Abie gave me the key and
told me to walk right in.

SOLOMON. [*Rises, goes to her.*] Mrs. Cohen—I vant you
to know Rosie. Miss Rosie Murpheski.

MRS. COHEN. [*Crosses to her.* ROSE MARY *rises.*] Miss
Murpheski! I am glad to know anybody what iss a friend
of Abie's.

SOLOMON. Sid down Mrs. Cohen. Make yourself homely.
[MRS. COHEN *sits on davenport.*] Oh, won't you lay off
your furs for a minute?

MRS. COHEN. No thanks, I have to be goink in a few minutes.

SOLOMON. [*Center.*] You von't feel the good of it.
What's the use of havin' furs if you can't feel them when
you go oud. [*Gets chair at back.*]

MRS. COHEN. I always wear somethink around me in the

house, ever since my operation— [SOLOMON *drops chair.*] don't I, Solomon?

SOLOMON. [*Puts chair Center, facing davenport. Paying no attention.*] Yes. Yes—just think, Mrs. Cohen, Abie has known Rosie ever since the Var.

MRS. COHEN. Ve can blame a lod of things on the Var, can't ve?

ROSE MARY. I hope you won't blame the War for me.

MRS. COHEN. Vat a nize pleasant blame. Did you go over?

SOLOMON. Dod's vhere she met Abie.

MRS. COHEN. Oh, you poor dear, what a lot of suffering you must have seen.

ROSE MARY. I did.

SOLOMON. Abie got shot in the Argonne. He laid in the hospital for weeks.

MRS. COHEN. I can sympathize with anybody in a hospital.

SOLOMON. [*Trying to stop her.*] Yes ve know, your appendix was amputated.

MRS. COHEN. You know, Miss Murpheski, it started with a little pain, right here. [*Indicating her abdomen.*] Or was it here—

SOLOMON. Make up your mind.

MRS. COHEN. Now come to think of it—

SOLOMON. Don'd think of it, Mrs. Cohen. Forged it!

MRS. COHEN. I vish I could.

SOLOMON. So do I. [*She looks at him. He smiles, changing the meaning.*] It would be so much better for you, Mrs. Cohen.

MRS. COHEN. That is just what Isaac says. [*She sighs.*] But I can't.

SOLOMON. [*To* ROSE MARY.] Isaac is Mrs. Cohen's husbands. He'll be here in a few minutes. You'll like him, von't she, Mrs. Cohen?

MRS. COHEN. Oh, yes, he's *just a husband*—

[ROSE MARY *is amused at their conversation. The doorbell rings.*]

SOLOMON. Now I vonder who dod can be?

MRS. COHEN. Abie, maybe, he gave me his key. I forgod to leave the door open maybe for him.

SOLOMON. [*Rises and puts chair back.*] I'll have to answer it. Sarah is so deaf she can't even hear the *doorbell anymore.* [*Doorbell rings again.*] Stop ringling. Can't you see I'm coming! [*He exits out into the hall Right Center.*]

MRS. COHEN. Miss Murpheski have you ever had an operation?

ROSE MARY. No, not yet.

MRS. COHEN. Then you've never taken ether.

ROSE MARY. No.

MRS. COHEN. Dey had to give me twelve smells! I was in

the hospital for three weeks. Oh vat a time I had. Miss Murpheski you should know vat I suffered after my appendix was oud.

ROSE MARY. I thought you suffered while it was in.

MRS. COHEN. And oud too.

[SOLOMON *enters followed by* ABIE.]

SOLOMON. Mrs. Cohen, Abie says Isaac will be right over.

ABIE. Will you give me the key to the front door, Mrs. Cohen, before we both forget it.

MRS. COHEN. Now vhere did I pud that key? [*Finds key on neck of dress.*] Oh, here it is.

SOLOMON. [ABIE *and* SOLOMON *exchange glances.*] Mrs. Cohen, vhy don'd you take off your fur?

MRS. COHEN. I'm a sight.

ABIE. We don't mind. Do we, Miss Murpheski?

ROSE MARY. I'm a sight myself. I haven't combed my hair since morning.

SOLOMON. Mrs. Cohen, vill you please take Rosie upstairs to the spare room.

ABIE. [*Up to arch Right Center.*] I'll show her where it is.

SOLOMON. [*Center.*] You'll do nothing of the kind. Mrs. Cohen, you know the house as vell as ve do.

MRS. COHEN. [*Rising and going up Right Center.*] Of

course I do. Come on, Miss Murpheski. You probably feel as dirty as I do.

[ROSE MARY *crosses to her.*]

ROSE MARY. [*To* SOLOMON.] I would like to wash my hands and powder my nose a bit.

SOLOMON. Run along, Rosie. [MRS. COHEN *leads the way.* ROSE MARY *follows her up the stairs.* ROSE MARY *takes* ABIE'S *hand in passing. Throws a kiss at him.* ABIE *looks after them.* SOLOMON *crosses to chair Left of table Left Center. Sits chuckling all the while—then says;*] Abie—kim a hare—tzurn-taten. [*His father's voice calls his attention.* ABIE *comes down and sits Right of table.*] Well, my son, you're getting some senses at last.

ABIE. You like her, Dad?

SOLOMON. She's a nice girl, Jewish and everything.

ABIE. [*Not so sure.*] Yeh!

SOLOMON. How much money has she got?

ABIE. Oh, I don't know exactly. Her father is comfortably fixed, that is all I know.

SOLOMON. And your father is comfortably fixed, too! [*Smiling knowingly.*]

ABIE. What do you mean?

SOLOMON. You like her, don'd you?

ABIE. Do I! [*This speaks volumes.*]

SOLOMON. Who could help it?

ABIE. Do you really like her, Dad?

SOLOMON. She's a nice girl. Didn't I told you to vait ven you brought all those girls around, those Christian girls? Didn't I say "Abie, vait—someday you'll meet a nize little Jewish girl." Didn't I say that?

ABIE. You did, Dad!

SOLOMON. Uh—Bahama, aren't you glad you vaited?

ABIE. I'm glad I waited for Rose Mary!

SOLOMON. [*Grabs his hand angrily, almost yelling at him.*] Please don'd call her Rose Mary. [*Smiles.*] She's Rosie!

ABIE. All right—Rosie! But I don't care what she is; it's the girl I like, not her religion.

SOLOMON. Sure—fine! You don'd care, but I care! We'll have no "Schickies" in this family. [*He hits table.*]

ABIE. You mean to say if Rosie were a Christian you wouldn't like her?

SOLOMON. Bud she isn't!

ABIE. Oh, piffle!

SOLOMON. [*Getting angry.*] Don'd you peefle me!

ABIE. I didn't mean it for you—

SOLOMON. [*Hitting table. Paying no attention to* ABIE'S *semi-apology.*] I von'd be peefled!

ABIE. [*Meekly.*] All right.

SOLOMON. No sir!

[ABIE *says nothing, sits with his hands deep in his pocket, hunched down in chair.*]

SOLOMON. Positivil! Ein umglik mit dem ziem meinen zoog ich azoi zoogt er azoi shut up. [ABIE *still says nothing.* SOLOMON *talks long strings of Jewish, then awakes to the fact that he is arguing against the wind; he looks at* ABIE. ABIE *pays no attention—seems lost in his own thoughts.*] Vhy don'd you say something?

ABIE. There is nothing to say.

SOLOMON. Don'd argue with me. You get a nice little Jewish girl and you don'd hang on to her.

ABIE. [*With double meaning.*] I'm hanging on to her all right!

SOLOMON. Yeh, all right vhy don'd you marry her qvick?

ABIE. Dad, have I your consent?

SOLOMON. Do you vant *me* to ask her for you?

ABIE. No. I can do that.

SOLOMON. Vell do it, and—if she says yes, I'll start you in some kind of a business. What would you like?

ABIE. I hate business.

SOLOMON. You'll need a business ven you start raising a fambly! Esk Rosie! She's got a common senses!

ABIE. [*Apprehensively.*] Say, Dad—don't mention anything about a family to Rose Mary.

SOLOMON. [*Grabs head angrily.*] Oi— Ich platz. Didn't I

just tell you not to call her dod Rose Mary. [*Smiles.*] She's Rosie!

ABIE. All right, Rosie! But say please don't mention anything about a family to her, will you?

SOLOMON. Vat's the matter? She pelieves in a fambly, don't she?

ABIE. [*Nervously*]. Why, I don't know. I've never asked her that.

SOLOMON. Vell, say, if she don'd, after you marry her make her change her mind.

ABIE. Well, it is just as well not to say anything to her about it anyhow.

SOLOMON. Sure! Ve know, don'd ve! [*Nudging* ABIE *in the side.*]

ABIE. [*Uncomfortably.*] Yes!

[MR. COHEN *enters Right Center. He is an undersized little man, very much stoop shouldered, slightly bald, and absolutely dominated by* MRS. COHEN. *He is the direct antithesis of his wife. She is beautiful big and loud. He is undersized, quiet and—retiring.*]

COHEN. Hello, Solomon! [*Down to* SOLOMON. *Shakes hands.*]

SOLOMON. [*Rising and going to* COHEN—*very excited.*] Isaac, my friend, congratulate me.

COHEN. What's the matter? Has somethink happened?

SOLOMON. [*Smiling blandly.*] You should esk me! You should esk me!

COHEN. [*Smiling too.*] I am esking you. Abie has somebody died and left him some money?

SOLOMON. Money—money—there are greater things in life than money.

COHEN. Vell, don't keep me in suspenses!

SOLOMON. Go on, boy—you tell him.

ABIE. [*Nervously.*] Why there is nothing to tell him yet—

SOLOMON. [*Angrily.*] Vot? Nothink to tell! Ain'd you going to esk Rosie to marry you?

ABIE. [*Nervously.*] Yes— [*Hesitating on the "yes" a bit.*]

SOLOMON. [*Mimicking him.*] Yes— Dod's no vay to feel.

COHEN. Rosie? Who iss it Rosie?

SOLOMON. [*Very expressively.*] Oi! You should see Abie's Rosie! Such a hair! Such a teeth! Such a figure!

COHEN. [*Reprovingly.*] Solomon!

SOLOMON. [*Turning again very angrily.*] And dot schlimiel he's known her since de Var! They should have been married with the childrens py this time.

ABIE. [*Looking toward the stairs.*] Ssh!

SOLOMON. [*Indignantly.*] I von't be shushed.

COHEN. Vhere is Rosie?

ABIE. She's upstairs with Mrs. Cohen.

SOLOMON. [*Almost weeping; slapping* COHEN, *nearly*

knocking him over.] Isaac, I love dod girl! She's vine vife for Abie! Und dod loafer he won't esk her yet.

COHEN. [*He walks sideways until he hits the davenport.*] Solomon, control yourself! Abie hasn't esked her yet, maybe she won't hab 'em. [*Sits on arm of davenport.*]

SOLOMON. [*Immediately forgetting his sadness.*] Vot! Nod marry my Abie! Look what's talking. Who could refuse my Abie. Ain'd he my son?

ABIE. [*Rises.*] Listen, Dad!

SOLOMON. [*Turning to* ABIE.] Vell, I'm listening!

ABIE. Do you like Rosie?

SOLOMON. Isaac, listen to him after all I have—

ABIE. [*Interrupting him.*] Now wait a minute!

SOLOMON. Oi! Such a talk!

ABIE. Do you want Rosie for a daughter-in-law?

SOLOMON. Do I vant a million dollars?

ABIE. All right, I'll ask her. But you are quite sure *you* like her?

SOLOMON. [*Smiling at* COHEN *blandly.*] Ain'd dod a son to hev?

COHEN. Vell, Solomon, you hev been hard to blease! I'll say dod for you! Abie has prought at least a dozen girls I've seen my own eyes with.

SOLOMON. But dey vere not Jewish!

[*As though this statement was the Alpha and Omega. At this* ABIE *gets a bit nervous again.*]

ABIE. [*A bit angrily.*] Well, I want you both to know that I'm not marrying Rosie because she's Jewish— [*Walks away to Left.*] I wouldn't care if she were Turkish!

COHEN. [*At the word "Turkish."*] Vell dod wouldn't be so bad!

SOLOMON. [*Looks sternly at* COHEN. *Pause. Turns to* ABIE. *Sternly.*] But I vould care!

ABIE. Then you don't like Rosie for herself. [*Up to him.*]

SOLOMON. Well, boy, I think I like her preddy vell, for vone day.

ABIE. [*The idea striking him.*] Then the longer you know her the better you'll like her.

[MRS. COHEN *enters coming down the stairs followed by* ROSE MARY. MRS. COHEN *is talking.*]

MRS. COHEN. And the doctor said he never saw a case like mine. My appendix was so small you could hardly see it! [ROSE MARY *smiles.* COHEN *rises and crosses to Right. Comes down Left of davenport and sits.*] Papa here. [*Motioning casually toward* COHEN.] Thought he was going to lose his mama. Didn't you, Papa?

COHEN. [*He is Right of davenport.*] Yes, Mama. Yeh, yeh—

SOLOMON. Rosie! [ROSIE *does not recognize her name, continues to be deeply interested in* ABIE *up Right Center.*] Rosie! [*Still does not turn. He calls louder.*] Rosie! [*He is so loud this time they* BOTH *turn at the noise.*

When they turn he smiles.] Rosie, don't you know your name?

ROSE MARY. Oh, I beg your pardon. [*She leaves* ABIE *and comes down Right Center.* SOLOMON *crosses to her.*]

SOLOMON. I vant you to meed a very dear friend of mine, Mr. Cohen, Mrs. Cohen's husband.

[COHEN *crosses to Left of davenport.*]

ROSE MARY. [*Holds out her hand which he takes.*] How do you do, Mr. Cohen?

COHEN. So this is Rosie! [*Takes her hand.*]

SOLOMON. [*Smiling delightedly.*] Is she the same I told you?

COHEN. Also, and more. It's a pleasure— [MRS. COHEN *pulls his coat-tail. He is looking at* ROSE MARY *full length. He looks at* MRS. COHEN *for a second. She pulls him onto the davenport.*] I'm sure, to meet you. [*Ad lib, to* MRS. COHEN.]

SOLOMON. You know, Rosie, ve vere talking aboud you while you vas gone.

[ABIE *eases to above table Left Center.*]

ROSE MARY. [*Turning to* SOLOMON.] How lovely! What were you saying?

SOLOMON. Ve vere saying vot a lucky man he would be, who god you.

ROSE MARY. Oh, thank you.

SOLOMON. If I was young enough—I vould try myself.

ROSE MARY. Oh, Mr. Levy, your blarney is wonderful!

[ABIE *crosses to Left of table Left Center.*]

SOLOMON. [*Immediately changing. Grabs his head.*] Please don'd say dod void to me. I never allow it to be used in my house.

ROSE MARY. Why! [*This is more an exclamation than a question. She is so surprised by the change.*]

SOLOMON. I had once dealings with a fellow named Murphy and what he didn't do to me. Every time I hear dot void blarney it reminds me of dot Irisher.

ROSE MARY. [*Nervously.*] Then you don't like the Irish?

SOLOMON. Could you like the Irish? I'm asking you?

ABIE. Dad!

SOLOMON. [*Turning to him.*] Vot's the matter?

ABIE. You don't have to get so excited about it.

SOLOMON. [*Gritting his teeth.*] I am not excited. [*Turning to* ROSE MARY.] Could you marry an Irishman?

ROSE MARY. [*Looking at* ABIE *with double meaning.*] No, I couldn't! [*Laughing.*]

SOLOMON. There! Vot did I told you? You know, Rosie — [*Thinking he has won the argument.*] Ven you marry, you get you a nize little Jewish boy what keep his Yom Kippur. [*He passes* ROSE MARY *over to* ABIE.]

ROSE MARY. I intend to.

SOLOMON. You hear dod, Abie? [COHEN *and* MRS. COHEN

listening to all this and smiling benignly upon ABIE *and* ROSE MARY *too.* COHEN *nudges* MRS COHEN *who nods as much as to say "It meets with my approval."*] She is going to marry a little Jewish boy, ain'd dod nize? [*He turns to* COHEN *for his approval.* COHEN *nods his head.* ROSE MARY *and* ABIE *go up to arch Left Center. They are a bit embarrassed but cannot help themselves.*]

MRS. COHEN. [*Rises.*] Come on, Papa! Ve hev to hev supper. [*Crosses to Center.*]

SOLOMON. You are goink to hev supper here! I should let you go home! Never!

COHEN. Bud, Solomon—

MRS. COHEN. Shud up, Isaac, didn't you hear vot Solomon said, he invited us.

COHEN. [*Melting immediately, he knows he had better.*] Oh, is dod so, tanks! [*Shaking* SOLOMON's *hand; goes up Right Center.*]

SOLOMON. Mrs. Cohen, you run and tell Sarah you are staying and if she don'd like it, you fix it yourself.

MRS. COHEN. Sarah won'd mind, she likes me. Ever since my operation, she likes to hear about it.

SOLOMON. Tell her again! [MRS. COHEN *exits door Left.*] It looks like a party! Yes? [*Beaming on them.*]

MRS. COHEN. [*Sticks her head through the door Left and yells for* COHEN.] Isaac! Come here vonce, I vant you! [*She immediately exits, knowing her word is law.*]

SOLOMON. Maybe she's got another appendicitus!

COHEN. I ain'd so lucky.

MRS. COHEN. [*Off Left.*] Isaac, come here, I want you.

COHEN. Oh, Mama! Always you want something. I vantcha—*I vantcha*— [*He rushes to Left door and exits. The doorbell rings.*]

SOLOMON. Now, who can dod be? [*Crosses up Right.*]

ABIE. Let Sarah answer the bell, Dad, you spoil her.

SOLOMON. She can't hear the pell!

ABIE. Then get somebody who can.

SOLOMON. And discharge Sarah?

ABIE. Certainly.

SOLOMON. [*Turns at the arch to speak.*] I know, Abie, bud if I discharge Sarah she can't get another job. [*He exits Right Center.*]

ROSE MARY. Oh, Abie, he's really a dear!

ABIE. Of course, he is, and so are you.

[*Looks around to see that no one is looking and takes* ROSE MARY *in his arms. He kisses her. As he does so,* SOLOMON *enters Right Center again, followed by the* RABBI. SOLOMON *motions the* RABBI *to be quiet;* SOLOMON *beams. The* RABBI *looks at the lovers in their embrace. He cannot understand the situation; he looks at* SOLOMON *gesticulating like a mad man, he is so happy.* SOLOMON *comes further down into the room;* ABIE *and* ROSE MARY *still hold the kiss.* SOLOMON *cannot contain himself any longer, so he yells, almost scaring the lovers to death.*]

SOLOMON. [*Looks at watch; counts five.*] Time!

[ROSE MARY *and* ABIE *jump as though shot.* RABBI *goes down Right of davenport.*]

ROSE MARY. Oh!

ABIE. [*Undertone.*] Dad!

SOLOMON. [*Beaming.*] Don't plush, Rosie! I kissed Abie's mama just the same vay vonce!

ROSE MARY. Oh, Mr. Levy! [*Goes to* SOLOMON'S *arms—embarrassed to tears.*]

SOLOMON. Call me Papa! [*He takes her in his arms. Her head is on his shoulder.*]

COHEN. [*Enters. To* RABBI.] Hello, Doctor.

SOLOMON. Isaac, my friend, Abie did it. [*Shakes* CO-HEN'S *hand, turning to* RABBI *as he does so.*] Didn't he did it Doctor Samuels? Didn't he did it?

RABBI. I don't know what you are talking about, Solomon.

SOLOMON. Didn't you see what I saw before we came into the room just now, vid Abie and Rosie?

RABBI. Oh, you mean the kiss?

SOLOMON. [*Turning to* COHEN *delightedly.*] You hear vod he say! He saw the same thing. Oh such a happiness! [*Crossing to the* RABBI.]

COHEN. [*Opens door Left and yells at the top of his voice.*] Mama! Quick! Abie did it! Abie did it!

ABIE. [*Embarrassed for* ROSE MARY; *also a little for himself.*] Dad, please!

[ABIE *and* ROSE MARY *come down Center. He takes her in his arms.*]

MRS. COHEN. [*Entering out of breath. She has on an apron as though cooking.*] Isaac, what iss it?

COHEN. Abie did it.

MRS. COHEN. [*Sees the* RABBI. *Crosses to Center.* COHEN *crosses to Left.*] Doctor Samuels, what is it?

SOLOMON. Mrs. Cohen [*Beaming.*] Abie asked her!

MRS. COHEN. [*Loudly.*] Oh! You sveet child! Ven you going to be married by the good Rabbi here?

ROSE MARY. [*To* ABIE'S *arms.*] Rabbi!

SOLOMON. Next week!

ROSE MARY. Abie!

SOLOMON. [*Interrupting.*] Oh, you can be ready by next week, Rosie! I'll get the trousseaus—the svellest in the city! I'll go to Greenbergs. He gives me a discount.

ABIE. But, Father—Rose Mary and I want to tell you—

SOLOMON. [*Incensed at the interruption.*] Young man, whose vedding iss dis?

ABIE. [*Now thoroughly going.*] It's mine!

SOLOMON. Den keep *quiet, I'll run it!*

[SOLOMON *and* MRS. COHEN *go to the* RABBI *in consulta-*

tion. ROSE MARY *in consternation is gathered into* ABIE'S *arms trying to pacify her.* COHEN *is in the seventh heaven of delight as*

THE CURTAIN FALLS

ACT TWO

SCENE: *Same as Act One. With the exception that the entire room is decorated with oranges. There are orange trees of all different sizes. Oranges in bunches hanging on the walls which are festooned with orange ribbons. The place looks like a veritable orange bower.*

TIME: *One week later.*

AT RISE: ROSE MARY *in her wedding dress steals into the living room from upstairs making sure no one is there, she is very mysterious about her movements. Then she goes to the telephone, picks it up and calls:*

ROSE MARY. Pennsylvania-6-5600. [*Then she looks around cautiously again.*] Yes, hurry please! [*There is a pause as she waits for the number.*] Hello, hello! [*She seems very agitated.*] Pennsylvania-6-5600. Information? Can you tell me if the 6.30 from Chicago is on time? [*She pauses.*] One hour late, but you think it will make up some of the time? Thank you. Goodbye. [*Hangs up, crosses to arch Right Center.*]

ABIE. [*Enters from Right stops, listening to* ROSE MARY, *placing his hat on table Right Center.*] Rose Mary! [*She turns and sees* ABIE; *almost shrieks.*] Why, what is it, dear?

ROSE MARY. You shouldn't see me in my wedding dress until we're married! It's bad luck! [*She almost weeps— together with her agitation over the telephone.*]

ABIE. [*Putting his arms around her soothingly.*] Nonsense, it's good luck to see you at any time.

ROSE MARY. I know, but we should be very careful. It might be true.

ABIE. [*Laughing.*] Well, I didn't see you in your wedding dress before we were married. You forget we've been married a week today. This is our anniversary. We're celebrating our wedding by being wedded again.

ROSE MARY. I forgot! Oh, Abie, it's been an awful week!

ABIE. I know it, dear! [*Holding her in his arms.*] But it will soon be over.

ROSE MARY. Abie, Father's train is an hour late.

ABIE. Good!

ROSE MARY. But they said they would probably make up some of the time.

ABIE. We mustn't delay the wedding a minute.

ROSE MARY. If my father arrives before the Rabbi marries us, both your father and my father will prevent it.

[*Down Center looking Left.*]

ABIE. [*To her; shakes her.*] Mrs. Abraham Levy, you speak as if you weren't married to me at all.

ROSE MARY. I know, Abie. But your father wouldn't be-

Act II

See page 53

lieve we've ever been married with only a minister offi-
ciating. [*Turns to him.*] Neither would my father. My
father won't even pay any attention to the Rabbi.
[*Crosses to davenport.*]

ABIE. But my father will. According to him, we'll be
married good and tight this time. And it is all his fault,
he has arranged every bit of it.

ROSE MARY. Then, please God, he doesn't find out I'm not
a little Jewish girl until the good Rabbi ties the knot.
[*Sits on davenport.*]

ABIE. Amen! [*Sits beside her.*]

ROSE MARY. The knot that we had tied a week ago, a little
tighter. Abie, I'm getting awfully nervous!

ABIE. Now don't worry, dear. Everything is going to be
all right.

ROSE MARY. What time is it?

ABIE. [*Looking at his watch.*] Six fifteen.

ROSE MARY. I hope Father's train doesn't make up any
time!

ABIE. In fifteen minutes you will be married to me for the
second time.

ROSE MARY. [*Fervently.*] I hope so!

SOLOMON. [SOLOMON *comes down the stairs. He is all
dressed for the wedding. He has on a suit a trifle large.
He walks down Center, pirouettes.*] Abie—Rosie—give
a look—a regular dandy!

[*They* BOTH *rise.*]

ABIE. Father, I told you to have that suit made smaller.

SOLOMON. [*Facing him.*] Vot? I paid fifty-nine dollars and ninety-eight cents for this suit. Und den you vont dot I should have some of it out? No, sir. I vant all I paid for. [*Faces Left.*]

ABIE. But, it doesn't fit!

SOLOMON. I don't vant it to fit.

ROSE MARY. Abie, it's lovely. [*Crosses to* SOLOMON.]

SOLOMON. You hear. That boy has no idea of the money. I could hire a suit but he says no, und I buy this to please him und den he ain't pleased yet.

ABIE. Yes I am, Dad. [*Crosses to Right of davenport.*]

SOLOMON. Fifty-nine dollars and ninety-eight cents to wear a suit for von night. I could hire a suit for three dollars und save fifty-six dollars and ninety-eight cents.

ROSE MARY. Never mind; you look wonderful.

SOLOMON. [*Holding out his arms.*] And how sveet you look! Oi! Such a bride! Abie, look at her. Look at her! Und den tank me!

ABIE. The Rabbi hasn't married us yet. [*Crosses to front of davenport.*]

SOLOMON. He'll soon be here! Oi! I hope nothink happens to his texes keb!

[ROSE MARY *goes up Right Center to arch.*]

ABIE. Father, please don't borrow trouble! I'm nervous enough.

SOLOMON. You're nervous! Vot do you tink I am? But I shall nod rest until I see you two lovers unided for life.

ABIE. Neither shall I.

SOLOMON. Unided you stand, divided you don'd.

ROSE MARY. [*Crossing down to* ABIE.] Abie and I are never going to be divided, are we, Abie?

ABIE. [*She is in his arms.*] I'll say we're not.

SOLOMON. Dod's de vay my childrens should speak up. Dod's de vay, Rosie! [*Crosses to Left Center.*] Vell, vod you tink of the decorations, you haven't said it yet. I did it all for you, Rosie.

ROSE MARY. They're beautiful.

SOLOMON. [*To Center.*] Does dod bring California back to you?

ROSE MARY. It certainly does. I love oranges.

SOLOMON. Now I'm glad now I couldn't get the blossoms. You know this is more of an economical idea. Ven the wedding is over, we can *eat* the fruit.

ABIE. [*Reprovingly.*] Dad!!

SOLOMON. [*Not getting the tone.*] Vod do I care for expenses, ven it's all for my little Rosie. I told Cohen this vedding vos goink to be the svellest blow-up in the Bronx. [*He stops for a second.*] I vonder if dos musicians have come yet? I ordered dem for a quarter past six. [*Crossing to Left.* ROSE MARY *up to arch Right Center.*]

ABIE. [*Looking at his watch.*] It's only that now!

SOLOMON. Den they should be here.

ABIE. [*Nervous and a bit impatient with his father's chatter.*] Oh, Dad, give them a chance! [*Crosses to him Left Center.*]

SOLOMON. I'm givink them money; why should I give dem chances, a business with chances, dey should be here playing already!

[ABIE *crosses down Right.* SOLOMON *moves chair at back to down Center.*]

ABIE. Not until after the ceremony, Dad. I'm too nervous for music just now! [*To Right Center.*]

SOLOMON. [*Teasing him.*] Abie! For why are you nervous?

ROSE MARY. [*Down to* ABIE.] Abie, isn't it time to begin?

SOLOMON. But, Rosie, your father isn't here yet.

ABIE. [*Nervously.*] His train is late.

SOLOMON. [*Sits in chair Left Center.*] Den ve'll vait for him.

ROSE MARY. No—no! [SOLOMON *looks at her in surprise.*] It's bad luck to wait, isn't it, Abie?

ABIE. Positively.

SOLOMON. [*Perplexed.*] Yeh, but who vill give the bride avay?

ROSE MARY. I'll give myself away!

SOLOMON. Oi! I never did hear of such a talk!

ABIE. I know how to get around it!

SOLOMON. Giving the bride away?

ABIE. Yes.

SOLOMON. Ven the Rabbi esks, who gives the bride avay, you speaks oud of your turn and says, "Nobody, I take her myself!"

ABIE. Just tell the Rabbi to omit that part of the ceremony.

SOLOMON. Vat, leave oud sometink, ven it costs me so much money for the decoratings?

ROSE MARY. [*Pleadingly; hugs* SOLOMON.] Please don't make us wait!

SOLOMON. [*Changing immediately.*] Abie! You see she can't vait!

ABIE. [*Crosses to door Right.*] I'm more impatient than Rosie!

SOLOMON. Never did I see such love. [*Doorbell rings.* ROSE MARY *and* ABIE *start nervously,* SOLOMON *smiles broadly. He rises.*] Rosalie, maybe dod is your papa, our very good friend Solomon Murpheski! I vond to shake his hands! [*Goes to arch Right Center and exits, going to door. Slight pause.* ROSE MARY *almost in tears.* ABIE *reassuringly embraces her.*]

ROSE MARY. [*Almost in tears.*] Abie!

ABIE. Don't weaken! If it's your father— [*She starts.*] We'll have to face it. That's all!

[*Voices are heard out in hall. They face up stage.*]

SOLOMON, MR. AND MRS. COHEN. Maziltof! [*Leads the way in from hall, followed by* COHEN *and* MRS. COHEN *who go to Left and Right end of table up Center respectively.* ABIE *is standing with his arm protectingly about* ROSE MARY *waiting for the blow to fall.*] Isaac, look! [*Coming down Center.*]

COHEN. A regular tscotska.

SOLOMON. [*Very proudly.*] *Ain'd* she a bride?

MRS. COHEN. [*Going down to* ROSE MARY.] My dear, your gown is beautiful!

COHEN. But, Mama, look vots in the gown.

MRS. COHEN. Isaac!!!!

[MRS. COHEN *gives him a hard look, and he goes up Left and brings a chair down to Left Center.*]

SOLOMON. Yess! [*Beaming—as doorbell rings again.*] Rosie, maybe dod is de papa!

[*He is delighted to think so.* ABIE *and* ROSE MARY *look almost frightened to death again.*]

COHEN. Ain'd her papa here yet? [*Sits Left Center.* MRS. COHEN *sits Right of him.*]

ABIE. No!

SOLOMON. Answer the door, Abie, and leave it open so the peoples can valk right in.

[ABIE *looks at* ROSE MARY. *She crosses herself surreptitiously.* ABIE *goes up to Right Center and exits.*]

MRS. COHEN. Ain'd you afraid to leave the door open?

SOLOMON. [*Center.*] Vid a vedding goink on? Nefer!
Always leave the door open for veddings and funerals!
It's stylish.

COHEN. Rosie, have you heard from the papa?

ROSE MARY. Yes, his train is an hour late.

MRS. COHEN. Musd ve vait an hour?

SOLOMON. Rosie von'd vait! [*Thinking this is a huge
joke.* ROSE MARY *doesn't pay much attention to their
chatter. She is back of the davenport looking apprehensively at the hall arch, thinking it might be her father.*]

MRS. COHEN. Vell, I don't blame her. It's bad luck! Ve
delayed our vedding fifteen minutes, und I always said,
dod'd de reason I god my appendicitis!

[ISAAC *puts hat under chair,* RABBI *enters Right Center
followed by* ABIE. RABBI *goes to shake hands with* SOLO-
MON. ABIE *goes back of davenport to* ROSE MARY.]

SOLOMON. [*Disappointed.*] Oh! I thought dod vos Rosie's papa! Hello, Doctor Samuels! Vell, I guess you is
as much importance.

RABBI. [*Center.*] Yes—I'm the one who does it.

SOLOMON. Vell, Doctor Samuels, do it vell!

RABBI. I will, Solomon, have no fear. [*Smiling.*] Well,
how are the Cohens tonight?

COHEN. [*Rises.*] Perfect. Couldn't be perfecter.

MRS. COHEN. [*Falls in chair.*] Isaac, speak for yourself!
I have my own feeling, vod you don'd know aboud.

[COHEN *is squelched and sits meekly.*]

ABIE. Doctor Samuels, hadn't we better start things?

RABBI. I'm ready! Rosie, where are your bridesmaids?

SOLOMON. They're upstairs vaiting. Go on up, Rosie, you've god to come down vid dem!

RABBI. Is her father here?

SOLOMON. No, his train is late.

RABBI. Then what is the hurry?

SOLOMON. Rose vonts to be married!

RABBI. Yes, of course. But who will give the bride away?

SOLOMON. That's just it!

MRS. COHEN. Isaac, you give the bride avay.

COHEN. Sure I don'd care.

SOLOMON. Sure, you don'd care. It don'd cost you noddings.

RABBI. Does that meet with your approval, Rosie?

ROSE MARY. [*Who is by now very nervous.*] Oh, yes, yes!

SOLOMON. Vell run along den, Rosie!

ROSE MARY. [*Picking up her skirts preparing to go.*] Goodbye, Abie. I'll meet you at the altar, if I'm lucky!

[*She rushes out and upstairs. They* ALL *look after her.* SOLOMON *goes up to Left of arch Right Center.* ABIE *in arch.* RABBI *looks after her; then crosses back of davenport to front of it.*]

SOLOMON. She's so afraid sometink is going to happen. I don'd know vod!

MRS. COHEN. She is nervous! All brides are! I remember I was dreadfully nervous. Vosn't I, Papa?

COHEN. Oh yes, Mama! Bud you soon god over your nervousness, Mama!

MRS. COHEN. A vedding is almost as bad as an operation.

COHEN. Concentrate, Mama, concentrate!

[RABBI *is looking around room in perplexity.* SOLOMON *sees him, he swells all up again. Comes down Center.*]

SOLOMON. Vell! Vod you tink? Some decorations, yes?

RABBI. Splendid, Solomon, but why all the oranges?

SOLOMON. All for Rosie! She comes from California! Ve couldn't ged the flowers, so I ged's the fruit! Real California *Navy* oranges. *Ain'd* dod an idea?

COHEN. Peautiful! Significance!

MRS. COHEN. Are they sveet?

SOLOMON. Yes, bud don't eat them! If you ged hungry please vait!

COHEN. Solomon, I don'd know how you thought of it. You're a genius!

SOLOMON. Vell, my Abie vill only be married vonce.

[ABIE *standing in arch Right Center glances at* SOLOMON *and exits.*]

COHEN. Doctor Samuels, vod shall I do ven you ask for the bride?

RABBI. Well—

MRS. COHEN. Isaac, don'd led them know how already dumb you are yet!

COHEN. What you mean how dumb I am yet?

[*Ad lib argument.*]

SOLOMON. Order—order—order—Mrs. Cohen, Isaac vonts to know!

MRS. COHEN. He's been married! He vent to his own vedding!

COHEN. I didn' vent. Dey took me. Doctor Samuels what shall I do when you esk for the bride?

RABBI. Don't get nervous, Isaac, it is very easy. You'll know exactly what to do when the time comes.

MRS. COHEN. Pud me somevhere so I can nudge him.

COHEN. Mama, I don'd vont to be nudged!

[MRS. COHEN *gives him a look.*]

SOLOMON. [*Center. Looks disgustedly at* COHENS.] Mrs. Cohen, I don'd tink anybody should be nudged at this vedding.

RABBI. [*Looking at his watch.*] It is time to begin, Solomon.

SOLOMON. I'll tell them to start the moosic! They should be earning their money already before! [*Crossing to door Left.*]

MRS. COHEN. Iss everybody here?

SOLOMON. You should see. I god it all fixed like a theatre, everybody is seated holding the front seats to see the show good.

RABBI. Isaac you go upstairs and wait for the bride! You bring her down on your arm.

[COHEN *gets hat and immediately starts for the stairs.*]

COHEN. The Bride! Sure! Fine!

MRS. COHEN. [*Follows him to arch.*] Und Isaac, vait outside the door! [COHEN *exits upstairs, very quickly.*] If I don't tell him, he goes right in by the bride. [*Exits Left.*]

[ABIE *enters.* SOLOMON *moves chair up Left and when* MRS. COHEN *exits, he puts other chair up.*]

RABBI. [*Going over to* ABIE *and slapping him affectionately on the shoulder.*] Good luck, son!

[*Music—"Oh, Promise Me"—starts softly as* RABBI *goes to door Left.* SOLOMON *goes to Left Center, and stands with back to the audience.*]

ABIE. [*Smiles at the* RABBI.] Thanks!

[RABBI *goes to* SOLOMON, *pats him affectionately, and exits Left.* SOLOMON *has been looking at* ABIE *affectionately, he goes up to him, puts his arm around him.* ABIE *gets hat from table Right Center and crosses to* SOLOMON.]

SOLOMON. My little Abie! Sure it seems like only yesterday, I vos vaiting for your mama, just like you are vaiting for Rosie now. My son, I hope you can keep Rosie by your side until your hair is white like mine!!! My Re-

becca didn't stay so long wid me. Only a little vhile—
bud no one couldn't take her place. I tink you lofe Rosie
the same way.

ABIE. [*Center.*] I do, Dad. I love Rosie better than my
life.

SOLOMON. Dod's the vay, Abie! Und I lofe Rosie too!

ABIE. I'm so glad of that, Dad! Will you always love her?

SOLOMON. Sure, why nod? Ain'd she Jewish and everything?

[*At this* ABIE *is squelched again. The music stops.* RABBI
enters.]

RABBI. [*To Left Center.*] Solomon, everything is all
ready and waiting. The best man is here!

SOLOMON. Iss it time for the moosic?

RABBI. Yes!

SOLOMON. [*Getting excited.*] Vait till I gife the high
sign! [*He goes to door Left and waves his hand franti-
cally to the orchestra which is off stage.*] Go on—start to
commence! Go on! Ve're vaiting. [*Music begins, the
wedding march, off Left.*] There! Now vod do ve do?

[*The music softens.*]

RABBI. Abie. [*Indicates* ABIE'S *hat, he puts it on.*] Now
come. [*Exit* RABBI *Left.*]

ABIE. Dad, I'm nervous as a cat!

SOLOMON. It vill soon be over. [*He slaps his back affec-*

tionately.] Don't be nervous! [ABIE *exits Left.* SOLO-
MON *is more nervous than* ABIE. *He goes to table up
Center, gets his hat, puts it on, starts out Left, then rushes
to the foot of stairs and putting his hand to his mouth,
calls.*] Isaac! Don'd forget to bring up the rear! Abie's
goink in now! Come on! [*He runs about like a madman.
All of this time the "Wedding March" is being softly
played off Left. The* SIX BRIDESMAIDS *are seen coming
down the stairs. Then a* LITTLE FLOWER GIRL *strewing
flowers in front of the bride,* ROSE MARY, *who comes
down the steps on* COHEN'S *arm. Her eyes downcast.* THE
BRIDESMAIDS *exit Left.* COHEN *and* ROSE MARY *with* LIT-
TLE FLOWER GIRL *in front of them, follow the* BRIDES-
MAIDS *off Left.* SOLOMON *looks about, to see that they
are all in.*] I guess dod's all! [*Puts on his hat and slowly
crosses to door Left. As* SOLOMON *gets to door, music
strikes up loudly. Very pleased, he exits same door, closing it behind him. The music is still heard playing through
the closed door. The room is empty. Only the music
which finally stops. There is another long pause. The
doorbell rings one short ring. Then there is another
pause. Then the bell rings again, a longer ring. Another
pause. Then a long definite ring. Then voice is heard with
a distinct brogue in the hall.*]

PATRICK. Come on in, Father. This must be the house.
[*He enters, hangs hat on tree, goes down Left.* PATRICK
MURPHY, ROSIE'S *father, enters the room, followed by*
FATHER WHALEN. PATRICK *is a big, burly Irishman, red-
faced, brawny. The kind who fights at the drop of a hat,
but if appealed to in the right way, would give his last*

dollar. FATHER WHALEN, *the priest, is a good-looking man of the scholarly type. Gentle, and kind. Irish, but of the esthetic type.*]

FATHER WHALEN. Patrick, we shouldn't enter a man's house without an invitation.

PATRICK. This is the house all right. Didn't the children outside the door say the wedding was to be here. [*As he starts away from* FATHER WHALEN, *he spies the decoration of oranges; he looks about the place, blinking his eyes to make sure he is not "seeing things."*] Father Whalen, do you see what I see?

FATHER WHALEN. [*Looks about the room. He is surprised, too.*] Yes!

PATRICK. [*Center.*] What do you see?

FATHER WHALEN. [*Smiles.*] I see oranges.

PATRICK. Dozens of them?

FATHER WHALEN. [*Surprised at this unusual feature.*] Why, yes!

PATRICK. [*In sudden fear.*] Glory be to God, Father, she's marrying a Protestant!

FATHER WHALEN. Don't jump at conclusions!

PATRICK. I'm going to get to the bottom of this! [*He yells. Through door Left.*] Oh, Rose Mary! Rose Mary!!

FATHER WHALEN. Take it easy, son, take it easy!

PATRICK. Take it easy, with all them oranges staring me in the face! Rose Mary! Rose Mary!! [*Going to door Right, opening it and calling.*]

FATHER WHALEN. Patrick! You know love has never been a respecter of religion!

PATRICK. Who said anything about love? I'm talking about them oranges! [*To* FATHER WHALEN.] I hate orange! 'Tis the color of the damned A.P.A.'s—Rose Mary! Rose Mary!

[*He goes up Right.* FATHER WHALEN *comes down to front of davenport.* PATRICK *goes to Center. The Left door flies open and* SOLOMON *enters, closing the door behind him. Pantomimes* PATRICK *to hush.* PATRICK *walks down to him.*]

SOLOMON. [*On entrance.*] Shh! Sh! Shush, shush, please be qviet! You're interrupting the whole works!

PATRICK. [*To* FATHER WHALEN, *seeing* SOLOMON *and getting his dialect.*] He's no A.P.A.

SOLOMON. [*Suddenly beaming.*] Is your name Murpheski?

PATRICK. [*Not getting him yet.*] What?

SOLOMON. Are you Solomon Murpheski?

PATRICK. [*Looking at* FATHER WHALEN *then back to* SOLOMON.] Say, are you trying to kid me?

SOLOMON. No. I'm expecting Solomon Murpheski.

PATRICK. My name is Patrick Joseph Murphy.

SOLOMON. Gewald!

PATRICK. Not Gewald—Murphy! And I'm looking for my daughter. Is she here?

SOLOMON. [*Making a face at the name* MURPHY.] Nobody by dod name is here. Voddo you vant?

PATRICK. I'm looking for the home of Michael Magee!

SOLOMON. [*Laughs.*] Michael Magee! Listen to him! Efeter I've been telling you—

PATRICK. What is your name?

SOLOMON. [*Proudly.*] Solomon Levy! Does dod sound like Michaels Magee?

PATRICK. Well, I'll tell the world it doesn't!

SOLOMON. Den please go vay!

FATHER WHALEN. Come, Patrick, I told you we were in the wrong house. [*Goes up to arch Right Center.*]

SOLOMON. [*Starts for the door Left.*] Absitivle! Close the door und lock id ven you go oud.

PATRICK. [*Following.*] Wait a minute!

SOLOMON. [*Impatiently.*] Oi, please be qvick! It vill soon be over. Isaac is giving the bride avay. Und I vont to see it. It's the first thing in his life he ever gave avay, I'm telling you.

[*Laughs heartily.* PATRICK *walks slowly down to him.*]

PATRICK. [*Laughs.*] I'm very sorry. But I'm looking for my daughter. She is to be married tonight to a young fellow by the name of Michael Magee. I thought this was the address she gave me.

SOLOMON. No, sir! A girl by the name of Rosie Murpheski is marrying my son, Abraham Levy.

PATRICK. Ah, I see! Oh, but would you mind telling me, what you are doing with all the A.P.A. decorations?

SOLOMON. Oh, you liked id?

PATRICK. I'm not saying anything about that. But it seems very funny to have oranges for decorations.

SOLOMON. Vell, I'll tell you why! The girl's from California!

PATRICK. [*Cutting him short.*] So's my daughter!

SOLOMON. Bud my son is marrying a Jewish girl!

PATRICK. My daughter is marrying an Irish boy!

SOLOMON. [*Almost shouting.*] My son isn't Irish!

PATRICK. Well my God! My daughter isn't Jewish!

FATHER WHALEN. Come, Patrick!

PATRICK. [*Turning to* FATHER WHALEN.] But, Father, where can Rose Mary be? [*Crossing up stage.*]

SOLOMON. Wait a minute! [*In terror.*] Did you say Rose Marys?

PATRICK. [*Coming close to him.*] Shure I said it! That's my daughter's name!

SOLOMON. [*Suddenly grabbing his head.*] Oi vey is mire. Do you suppose it could be true?

PATRICK. [*Looking at him in amazement.*] What's the matter, are you having a fit?

SOLOMON. [*Pays no attention to* PATRICK, *but starts for*

door Left, yelling at the top of his lungs.] Vait a minute!
Stob id! Vait a minute! Stob it!

VOICE. [*Off Left.*] Mas ameah, hoosen veim ha calo!

[*As* SOLOMON *gets to the door, the music starts up, which
denotes the end of a Jewish ceremony.* GUESTS *cry "Masseltof," music plays.*]

SOLOMON. [*Holding his head.*] It's too late! It's too late!
[*He staggers into chair down Left.*]

PATRICK. What's that? Sounds like a riot!

[COHEN *enters Left. Does a wild sort of a dance.*]

COHEN. Solomon, did you see me give the bride avay?

SOLOMON. Vhere is Abie?

COHEN. He'll be here in a minute. Everybody is kissing
the bride. Und, believe me, Solomon, she is some bride!
I hated to give her avay! [*Crosses to Left Center.*]

PATRICK. [*To* FATHER WHALEN.] There is something
wrong here?

COHEN. [*Seeing him; crossing to him.*] Oh, is it a detective, vatching the vedding presents?

PATRICK. [*Turns to him.*] I'm no detective! I'm a contractor!

SOLOMON. Oi! Oi! The contractor! [*Holds his head.*]

COHEN. [*Advances.*] Oh, you're the papa?

PATRICK. What do you mean, the papa?

COHEN. Don't you know bot iss it, a papa?

PATRICK. [*Raising his fist.*] Don't you "papa" me!

FATHER WHALEN. [*Softly.*] Control yourself, Patrick! [*Crosses down Right of davenport.*]

SOLOMON. Oi! Patrick!

COHEN. Abie heard the doorbell ring und he thought it vos the papa. He sent me on ahead to see for sure.

PATRICK. Abie! And who in the hell is Abie?

COHEN. He's your new son-in-law!

PATRICK. [*Crosses to Left of davenport. To* FATHER WHALEN.] Did you hear that, Father? Abie! My new son-in-law! Well, that name better have an O or a Mac stuck in front of it!

COHEN. A Mac or an O in the front of a beautiful name like Levy?

PATRICK. [*Crosses down to* FATHER WHALEN.] My God! Did you hear that other name, Father? Abie Levy, my new son-in-law!

FATHER WHALEN. Sit down, Patrick, sit down!

[PATRICK *and* FATHER WHALEN *ad lib. both shaking heads and arguing, sit on davenport.*]

COHEN. And a fine boy he is too! He met Rose Marys when the Var vas here.

SOLOMON. Oi! Oi!

COHEN. Solomon, for why do you do dod? Oi! Oi!

[MRS. COHEN *enters Left. She is all aglow.*]

MRS. COHEN. [*To* SOLOMON.] Vod a vedding! Solomon, you have did yourself proud for vonce.

SOLOMON. Oi! Oi!

MRS. COHEN. Vod's the matter? Iss the expense worrying you already yet?

COHEN. [*Now thoroughly alarmed at* SOLOMON'S *distress.*] Mama, he's been doink dod since I came in, after the wedding.

MRS. COHEN. Solomon, heve you god a pain?

SOLOMON. I've god a sometink. I didn't vont, but now I've god it!

MRS. COHEN. That's the way I felt too about my appendix.

SOLOMON. It ain't my appendixes! I vish it vas!

MRS. COHEN. Solomon! If you vished it vas, you vish it vasn't! I know, I had the operation. Didn't I, Papa? [*She goes up.*]

COHEN. [*Center.*] Yes, Mama!

[*All this time* PATRICK *is looking on as though he would like to wring them* ALL *by the necks.*]

FATHER WHALEN. Well, Patrick, if our Rose Mary has married this boy, we'll have to make the best of it!

COHEN. Sure! They are crazy aboud each other. Never did I see such love. [*Crosses to* PATRICK.]

SOLOMON. They are both crazy!

COHEN. Solomon, Rosie is a wonderful girl. I vould take her in a minute. [*Crosses back to Center.*]

MRS. COHEN. Isaac! [*She swings about her fan, just grazing* COHEN'S *face.*]

COHEN. [*Covering himself.*] Vouldn't ve, Mama? [*Crosses to* MRS. COHEN. *Enter* RABBI *Left.*]

MRS. COHEN. I vould take her in a minute, vouldn't ve, Papa? [BOTH *go up Left.*]

SOLOMON. I'd sell her for a nickel!

PATRICK. [*Rising crosses to Center.*] You don't have to! I'm going to take her away for nothing.

SOLOMON. Oi! If you vould do me such a favor!

COHEN. But, Solomon, you had the Rabbi marry them yourself, for vhy have you changed?

SOLOMON. Esk him! [*Pointing to* PATRICK.]

COHEN. [*Crosses to* PATRICK.] Do you know?

PATRICK. I have a sneaking suspicion I do! [*Doubles up his fist.*]

COHEN. [*Crosses to* MRS. COHEN.] Mama, I don'd like dose sneaking suspiciousness!

[RABBI *goes to* PATRICK.]

RABBI. Are you Rosie's father?

PATRICK. *Rosie's* father? [*Turning to* FATHER WHALEN.]

SOLOMÓN. Oi! Oi!

RABBI. [*Center.*] Why, Solomon, what is the matter, has something happened?

SOLOMON. [*Pointing to* PATRICK.] Look at him! And ask me! I shall die from shame! His name's Murphy!

PATRICK. [*In a rage.*] You'll die for shame at looking at me! Shure, you won't be able to see me, you won't be able to see anybody—you won't have room enough to open your eyes, your poor little abbreviated excuse for an apostrophe! [*Starts for* SOLOMON, FATHER WHALEN *stops him.*]

SOLOMON. [*Rising, to* PATRICK.] I didn't hear a word you said, but I'll get even for it!

RABBI. Solomon, don't do anything rash.

SOLOMON. Dod little Irisher! Marrying my son Abie against his vill. No vonder, she vouldn't vait. She vas afraid he'd back oud. The—the—the little—Irish A.P.A.

[*He exits Left quickly.* PATRICK *starts right after him;* FATHER WHALEN *holding his arm.*]

PATRICK. Let me loose, Father—let me loose.

FATHER WHALEN. Patrick, where are you going?

PATRICK. [*Breaking away at the door Left.*] I'm going after that little runt and make him eat those words along with every damned orange in this place!

[*Exits Left;* FATHER WHALEN *crosses to front of davenport.*]

COHEN. Come on, Mama! Ve god to help Solomon. [*Starting after* PATRICK.]

MRS. COHEN. Isaac! Don'd bud in. If you come between them you'll get hit both vays! [*She exits Left.*]

COHEN. [*Following her.*] When I get through with that Irishman, I'll make him eat all the oranges in California.

[FATHER WHALEN *and* RABBI *look at each other for a second, then they smile.* RABBI *crosses to Left of davenport.*]

MRS. COHEN. [*Off Left.*] Isaac! Isaac!

FATHER WHALEN. It looks like war between the Murphys and the Levys.

RABBI. Yes, I pity the young folks!

FATHER WHALEN. So do I. They are going to have their hands full. Poor Rose Mary!

RABBI. I feel sorry for Abie, too. He's a fine lad.

FATHER WHALEN. And Rose Mary's a wonderful girl. But what are we going to do about it?

RABBI. Seems to me, it's a little too late to do anything.

FATHER WHALEN. Yes, there is no use locking the barn door after the mare has gone. You married them, didn't you?

RABBI. Yes, and Solomon, asked me to tie the knot good and tight.

[*He smiles at this.* FATHER WHALEN *laughs too.*]

FATHER WHALEN. [*Looking at* RABBI, *closely.*] You know, your face is very familiar.

RABBI. I have been thinking the same of yours. You live here in New York?

FATHER WHALEN. No! California. I came on with Patrick for Rose Mary's wedding. [RABBI *indicates davenport.* FATHER WHALEN *sits and then the* RABBI *sits.*] Have you ever been in California?

RABBI. No—never west of Pittsburgh!

FATHER WHALEN. And I have never been east, except during the War. I went over there!

RABBI. I went over there too!

FATHER WHALEN. Maybe that's where we met.

RABBI. Most likely. That is where Abie and Rosie met— Abie did his bit. He was quite a hero.

FATHER WHALEN. Wounded?

RABBI. Very badly!

FATHER WHALEN. Shure, I have comforted a great many boys of your faith in their last hours when there wasn't a good rabbi around.

RABBI. And I did the same thing for a good many boys of your faith—when we couldn't find a good priest.

FATHER WHALEN. We didn't have much time to think of any one religion on the battle fields.

RABBI. I'll say not!

FATHER WHALEN. Shure they all had the same God above them. And what with all the shells bursting, and the shrapnel flying, with no one knowing just what moment death would come, Catholics, Hebrews and Protestants alike forgot their prejudice and came to realize that all faiths and creeds have about the same destination after all.

RABBI. [*Shaking his head.*] True. Very true.

FATHER WHALEN. Shure, we're all trying to get to the same place when we pass on. We're just going by different routes. We can't all go on the same train.

RABBI. And just because you are not riding on my train, why should I say your train won't get there?

FATHER WHALEN. Exactly!

RABBI. You know [*Rises.*] I wish I could remember where I met you.

FATHER WHALEN. [*Rises.*] I feel the same way. However, as long as we both feel that we have met before, we're old friends. My name's Whalen. John Whalen. [*Holding out his hand cordially.*]

RABBI. And mine is Samuels! Jacob Samuels! [*Taking* FATHER WHALEN'S *hand, clasping it warmly.*]

FATHER WHALEN. John Whalen and Jacob Samuels! [*Laughs.*] Shure, 'tis almost as bad as Murphy and Levy!

RABBI. [*Laughing too.*] Yes, except that we're not married! [*They* BOTH *laugh heartily at this.*]

[PATRICK *and* SOLOMON *heard quarrelling off Left.* BRIDESMAIDS *scream and rush on to* RABBI; *where he tries to pacify them.* ROSE MARY *dashes out of door Left.*

She stops on seeing FATHER WHALEN. *Goes to him, throws herself into his arms.*]

ROSE MARY. Oh, Father Whalen!

FATHER WHALEN. There—there—child!

ROSE MARY. Can't you do something with Father? He's gone mad!

FATHER WHALEN. Such a pretty bride too! [*He looks around at the* GIRLS.] Faith, dear, you look frightened to death!

ROSE MARY. I have reason to be, Father! You ought to hear Abie's father and my father fight! Oh, such language!!

RABBI. Girls, wait in here, out of the way. It is just as well to keep out of sight of both fathers. Don't you think so, Father Whalen? [*The* GIRLS *exeunt with bit of chatter Left Center.*]

FATHER WHALEN. I do that! Shure, there's no use waving a red flag at a bull, unless you want more trouble.

[RABBI *closes doors after them, and remains up Left Center.*]

ROSE MARY. We couldn't have any more trouble!

RABBI. Oh, yes you can, my child—much more than this!

[ABIE *enters on the run; he stops on seeing* ROSE MARY; *takes a deep breath of relief.*]

ABIE. Oh!—I thought you had gone! [*Goes to her.*]

ROSE MARY. Isn't it awful? [*Crosses to* ABIE.]

ABIE. It's worse than I expected!

FATHER WHALEN. [*Right Center.*] Is this Abie?

ROSE MARY. Oh, pardon me, Father—I thought you'd met him! Abie, this is Father Whalen.—Father brought him all the way from California to marry us!

FATHER WHALEN. [*Holds out his hand as* ABIE *hesitates, before he sees* FATHER WHALEN *is so cordial.*] I'm glad to know you, Son!

ABIE. Father Whalen, I'm glad to know *you!*

RABBI. Where are the fond fathers? [*Loud ad lib off Left.*]

SOLOMON. [*Off Left.*] I tell you, don't push!

PATRICK. [*Also off Left. A growl.*]

FATHER WHALEN. Ah! [*Crosses to front of davenport.*]

ABIE. There they are.

ROSE MARY. Oh, dear!

ABIE. It's all your father's fault, if he hadn't come, everything would have been all right!

ROSE MARY. It is not my father's fault! It's your father's! I never saw such a man!

[FATHER WHALEN *turns away Right, smiling.*]

ABIE. My father is wonderful, he is just a little stirred up right now, that is all!

ROSE MARY. *All!* [*Turning away; crosses to front of*

davenport.] If he is only stirred up now, what is he like when he's really mad?

FATHER WHALEN. Here—here! Don't you two start to fight too! [*Pats* ROSE MARY *on the shoulder.*]

RABBI. That is just what the two fathers would like!

ABIE. [*Crosses to her.*] There—there—Rose Mary dear! Don't cry!

ROSE MARY. [*Crying.*] But your father said he'd sell me for a nickel!

[FATHER WHALEN *goes to Right of davenport, crosses Center to* RABBI.]

ABIE. [*Taking her in his arms.*] But you don't belong to my father, you belong to me! And I wouldn't sell you for the whole world with a fence around it!

[FATHER WHALEN *and the* RABBI *exchange glances and smile.*]

ROSE MARY. And my father said he was going to take me away from you and have the marriage annulled. He says that no rabbi cuts any ice with him!

ABIE. Well, the rabbi didn't marry him, he married us!

SOLOMON. [*Runs in to Center; stops.*] Abie, take your arm avay from her!

PATRICK. [*Entering after* SOLOMON; *stops too, Left Center.*] The marriage isn't legal!

SOLOMON. No, ve just found out that you ain'd married at all!

RABBI. [*Down Left.*] I beg your pardon. I have married a great many people—I know my business!

SOLOMON. No reflection, Doctor Samuels! It ain'd your fault this vone didn't took!

ABIE. What do you mean we are not married?

PATRICK. Her name isn't Murpheski! It's Murphy. Murpheski!! [*Making a face.*] And another thing—that license you got isn't legal with that name on it!

SOLOMON. [*Smiling delightedly.*] You see! Doctor Samuels, you married Rose Murpheski—dhere ain'd no Rose Murpheski, so dhere ain'd no merriage! Oi! Vod a relief!

PATRICK. Rose Mary—take off that dress and veil! I am going to take you home!

SOLOMON. I'll send you a letter of tenks for it!

PATRICK. [*Looking down belligerently on him.*] I don't want anything from you but silence, and plenty of that!

SOLOMON. All right! All right!

PATRICK. [*Turns back to* ROSE MARY.] Rose Mary! [*She hasn't moved from* ABIE'S *side.*]

ABIE. [*Holding her in his arms.*] She isn't going with you or anyone else.

SOLOMON. Abie, don'd be foolish. You ain'd married!

ABIE. Yes we are!!

SOLOMON. Bud id didn't took! Esk anybody! They'll

tell you the same thing! You married Rosie Murpheski. She ain'd!

RABBI. I'm afraid there might be some truth in what your father says, Abie!

ROSE MARY. We are married whether you like it or not! Aren't we, Abie?

ABIE. Yes, dear, and if this marriage didn't take—

SOLOMON. I von'd let you merry her again!

ABIE. You can't prevent it!

PATRICK. But I can!!

ABIE. Well, I married Rose Mary Murphy just one week ago today in Jersey City!

[ABIE *takes* ROSE MARY *in his arms.* SOLOMON *grabs his head.*]

SOLOMON. Oi!! I nefer did like dod town! [*Up Center.*]

PATRICK. [*To Left Center.*] Rose Mary, is this true?

ROSE MARY. Yes.

SOLOMON. Oi, such a headache!

PATRICK. Were you married by a priest?

[ROSE MARY *frightened—looks at* ABIE.]

ABIE. No. By a Methodist minister!

SOLOMON. It's gettink worse!

PATRICK. Then you are not married!

ABIE. Well, try and take her away from me!

PATRICK. If you thought you were married so good and tight last week, why did you do it over again?

SOLOMON. To make it vorser!

[SOLOMON *and* PATRICK *look at one another as if to start another fight.*]

ABIE. To satisfy my father.

SOLOMON. [*Getting furious.*] To satisfy me! Say, do you tink I am satisfied? Look at me!

PATRICK. [*Shouting, starting toward* SOLOMON.] *You* have nothing on me!

[SOLOMON, *frightened, goes to the* RABBI, *his hand on his heart.*]

FATHER WHALEN. [*Crosses to* PATRICK.] Patrick, as I told you before, you'd better make the best of it! The children have done all they could to satisfy both fathers.

PATRICK. Did they try to satisfy me? No! They get a Methodist minister first and a rabbi next—would I let a minister or a rabbi marry me?

FATHER WHALEN. Well, marriages by ministers and Rabbis are as legally binding as by priests or others!

PATRICK. They are not married!

ROSE MARY. [*Crying.*] Abie!

SOLOMON. I'm going to phone my lawyer! [*He starts for the door Left yelling.*] Cohen! Oh, Isaac!!

[PATRICK *follows him.* SOLOMON *exits.*]

PATRICK. [*To* ROSE MARY.] Get into your street clothes,

young lady. Father Whalen you see that she doesn't run away with him! I'm going after this poor fish and see what his lawyer has to say. They're not going to put anything over on me. [*Exits Left.*]

[*This leaves* RABBI, FATHER WHALEN, ROSE MARY *and* ABIE.]

ROSE MARY. [*Crying.*] Abie!

ABIE. What is it, dear? [*Trying to soothe her.*]

ROSE MARY. He doesn't believe we are married. He says it didn't take!

ABIE. But we are!

ROSE MARY. Oh, I told you we should have been married by a priest in Jersey City!

ABIE. Your father wouldn't be satisfied no matter who married us!

RABBI. [*Down Left.*] Father Whalen, I wouldn't suggest it, but as long as the young folks have made a business of getting married, I don't think it would do any harm to marry them again in her faith, do you?

FATHER WHALEN. I don't think so!

ROSE MARY. Father Whalen, would you? [*Crosses to him.*]

FATHER WHALEN. Where is the telephone?

ABIE. On the table! [*Indicates telephone.*]

FATHER WHALEN. I must get permission from my superior. [FATHER WHALEN *goes to telephone. Looks in address book for number. Then takes telephone.*]

ABIE. [*Crosses to him.*] But Doctor Samuels, why all this red tape?

RABBI. [ROSE MARY *goes to left of* FATHER WHALEN. *Up left.*] Every great institution must have organization, my boy, and we must respect their rules and regulations.

FATHER WHALEN. Give me Vanderbilt zero, two, three, four. That's right. Vanderbilt zero, two, three, four.

ROSE MARY. [*Nervously.*] Suppose your superior says no?

ABIE. [*To* ROSE MARY.] Suppose he isn't in?

FATHER WHALEN. Sssh— Hello—Vanderbilt zero, two, three, four? Is his Grace, the Archbishop in? Father Whalen from California, speaking. I'm sorry to trouble, but it's a very serious matter. Yes, yes, I must speak to him personally.

ROSE MARY. Tell him to hurry. Father will be here any minute!

RABBI. Father Whalen, there is a phone extension in the other room. You had better talk from it.

ABIE. But they are liable to want to use this one, and then they'll hear!

RABBI. I'll guard this phone, until the matter is settled one way or the other. [*To* ABIE.] Show Father where it is!

ABIE. This way, Father Whalen. [*Up to arch Left Center and exits.*]

RABBI. Hurry, you haven't much time.

FATHER WHALEN. [*Starts for arch Left Center.*] Come, Rose Mary! [*Turns in doorway.*] And if his Grace says yes, I'll tie the charmed knot so tight, it'll make you dizzy! [*Exits Left Center.*]

ROSE MARY. Doctor Samuels! Say a prayer for us.

RABBI. What will I say?

ROSE MARY. Say please God, make the Archbishop say yes. [*She exits.*]

RABBI. All right! [RABBI *closes door with a satisfied smile on his face.*]

MRS. COHEN. [*Enters Left; sees* RABBI.] Nefer did I see such a night! [*Sits on davenport.*] Nefer was I so tired! Oh dear! If my appendix wasn't out, I know I'd have it again!

RABBI. [*Down to* MRS. COHEN.] You mustn't worry about it. Everything is going to be all right!

[PATRICK *enters left. He looks around.*]

PATRICK. Where is my daughter?

RABBI. I think you told her to change her dress.

PATRICK. [*Center.*] Oh, she has gone to do it?

RABBI. You told her to, didn't you?

PATRICK. Where's the telephone in this house? I want to make reservations for California. I'm going to get out of this town on the first train and take me daughter with me!

RABBI. [*Goes to telephone.*] I'll get your number for you, Mr. Murphy. What road do you want to go by? The Penn?

PATRICK. The fastest road out of New York, and the soonest. [RABBI *takes receiver off and listens.*] What's the matter, won't Central answer?

RABBI. The line's busy!

PATRICK. You never can get a number when you want it! [*Starts for telephone.*] Here, give me that phone. I'll show you how to get it!

RABBI. No, no, Mr. Murphy—I insist on getting your number for you!

PATRICK. [*Ad. lib.*] I know but—

RABBI. There is someone speaking now, and we must not disturb them!

PATRICK. But if you'll allow—

RABBI. It would not be the right thing to do!

PATRICK. Yes, but if you'll—

RABBI. You wouldn't want to be disturbed, would you?

PATRICK. [*Turns away Center, disgusted.*] Ah!

RABBI. Central—give me Penn—six, five, six hundred.

PATRICK. Whoever it is, by this time they should be through talking!

RABBI. All right, thank you! [*Hangs up.*]

PATRICK. What's the matter now?

RABBI. The line's busy!

PATRICK. [*In rage.*] Oh, I'll never get out of this damn town!

[RABBI *crosses to arch Left Center.* SOLOMON *enters Left, followed by* COHEN.]

SOLOMON. Oo—ah—

COHEN. Oo-ah—oo!

SOLOMON. [*To* RABBI.] My lawyer says dod no matter vod I say, dhey are married so tight, it would make your head curl! [*Sits in big chair Left.*]

MRS. COHEN. Vod you tink! Didn't you tell Doctor Samuels to tie a good knot?

SOLOMON. [*Almost a scream.*] I should be so foolish! Oi! Oi!

PATRICK. [*Bounds across room to* SOLOMON *and just misses tramping on* COHEN, *who is in the way.*] If you don't stop saying Oi, Oi, you'll drive me to drink!

[PATRICK *turns, looks at* COHEN, *who frightened, crosses and sits Left of* MRS. COHEN. *As* PATRICK *continues to look at him,* MRS. COHEN *passes* COHEN *to Right of her and then looks defiantly at* PATRICK.]

SOLOMON. Did you hear that I'll drive him to drink! I'd like to drive you to something for wishing an Irish wife on my Abie!

PATRICK. Wishing it on him! The devil take him and all his.

RABBI. Ssh! Ssh! You know what it says in the Scriptures about family quarrels?

PATRICK. Family quarrels! Do I look like a member of this family? [*He looks around at them.*] No, and my daughter isn't going to be. Thank heaven, she wasn't married by a priest!

RABBI. And would that make any difference to you, Mr. Murphy?

SOLOMON. Dod's vhere he is lucky! He can do something widout fear or trembling. Bud vid me! [*Pointing to* RABBI.] You tie the knot and I'm tied to it!

PATRICK. I'm going to untie that knot, don't you worry!

SOLOMON. Worry if you untie it? If you please, I'll be very much obliged.

PATRICK. [*Goes to telephone.*] I don't want you to be anything but out of my life. Penn six, five, six hundred and don't you tell me the line's busy!

ABIE. [*Off Left Center.*] With this ring I do thee wed.

[RABBI *opens the door, disclosing wedding party*—FATHER WHALEN'S *voice is heard coming out clear and strong.*]

FATHER WHALEN. I now pronounce you man and wife. "Those whom God hath joined together, let no man put asunder."

[*As this is heard,* SOLOMON *comes to; he listens as though he cannot believe his ears.* PATRICK *is spellbound for the second, too.*]

PATRICK. My God! They've done it again!

[SOLOMON *turns, looks up at Left Center door, where is the picture of* ABIE *and* ROSE MARY *with* FATHER WHALEN *between them, the* BRIDESMAIDS *grouped around them, collapses in chair as*

THE CURTAIN FALLS

ACT THREE

ACT THREE

SCENE: *In* ABIE'S *and* ROSE MARY'S *little modest apartment.*

It is small and not elegantly furnished, but everything shows that a woman's hand has tastefully arranged everything.

There is a door direct Center at back, which leads into a foyer. Another door Center at back of foyer leads to the hall outside. A door down Right leads into the dining room. A window up Right. Another door up Left leads into the bedroom. There is a table Left Center with a chair on either side of it. A console with mirror above it, is down Left. A Christmas tree stands in the upper Right corner. Other furniture to dress the room.

There is a small table with a chair between Right door and window; a service table Left of the Center arch; a chair above the console down Left.

TIME: *It is Christmas Eve. One year later than Act Two.*

DISCOVERED: ABIE *and* ROSE MARY *are discovered. She sitting on chair just Left of Christmas tree.* ABIE *kneeling Left of her. She is holding a baby. The moonlight is streaming through the window Right, on them. All lights*

are out. ROSE MARY *is singing an Irish Lullaby*
"Too-ro-la too."
Together, they rise, and walk slowly to door,
Left, she singing softly. She goes out. ABIE
looks after her for a second, then turns on
lights.

ROSE MARY. [*Re-enters.*] Oh, I hope that baby sleeps
now.

ABIE. So do I. Hurry up, dear. [*Gets up on chair at tree.*]

ROSE MARY. Well, what do you want next? [*Holding
two ornaments up to him.*]

ABIE. Where's the star that goes on the top?

ROSE MARY. [*Getting it from table Left Center.*] Here
it is. [*She takes it over to him, he puts it on the highest
part of the tree. They kiss.* ABIE *gets off chair.*]

ABIE. The star of Bethlehem! Only we haven't any Wise
Men to see it!

ROSE MARY. This is the baby's Christmas tree, star and
all. [ABIE *gets off chair.*]

ABIE. Of course it is! So we should worry about the
Wise Men, eh what? [*They embrace.*]

ROSE MARY [*Goes over to the table, picks up another ornament which she takes back to* ABIE.] Say, Abie, did
your father ever have a Christmas tree for you?
[*Crosses to the table.*]

ABIE. My father, a Christmas tree? [*He laughs.*]

Act III

See page 95

ROSE MARY. Christmas wouldn't be Christmas to me without a tree.

ABIE. Well, my father doesn't believe there is such a day in the year.

ROSE MARY. [*Handing him another ornament.*] Didn't you ever get things?

ABIE. [*Putting it on the tree.*] You mean presents? [*Kiss.*]

ROSE MARY. Yes.

ABIE. Not directly from Father. But I found out later that he used to give Sarah money to get things for me, so I would have toys and things. Like the other boys.

ROSE MARY. You know, Abie, I can't understand. Our fathers seemed to love us so much, yet they won't forgive us for marrying.

ABIE. [*Gets down from the chair and puts his arm around her.*] Now, don't start to worry again about that. You are not strong enough yet. Aren't we happy?

ROSE MARY. Oh, Abie! [*Looking up into his face lovingly.*] But you worry too!

ABIE. Oh, I know it. But every time I do, I say to myself, "Well, old boy, you've got the dearest, [*Kiss.*] sweetest, [*Kiss.*] wife in the world, so why worry?"

ROSE MARY. That's right, we have each other.

ABIE. Don't forget our family, too!

ROSE MARY. [*Running to the door Left.*] Oh, Abie, I

put the baby's bottle of milk on the electric stove to heat, and forgot all about it. I bet I've broken another bottle. I'm always breaking them. [*She tiptoes off.*]

[ABIE *sings "Too ra loo ra." As she shuts the door. The door bell rings. He goes to the door Center. As he opens the outside door in the foyer,* MR. *and* MRS. COHEN *are there. They enter.* MRS. COHEN *first,* COHEN *behind so close he cannot be seen until she steps aside.* COHEN *pulls cane out of coat and frightens* MRS. COHEN.]

ABIE. Well, look who's here! Come in, Mrs. Cohen! How are you, Mr. Cohen?

MRS. COHEN. Hello, Abie! [*Bustling in with her regular spirit.*] Ve vere just goink home from the theatre und I said to Isaac come on, let's go see Abie and Rosie a minute. Didn't I, Papa?

COHEN. You did, Mama.

ABIE. I'm glad you did. Won't you take off your things?

COHEN. Yes, Abie!

MRS. COHEN. Sure, why not? Isaac! Be a gentleman once in a while! [*She stoops and* COHEN *takes off her coat, and places it off Center.*] Where's our little Rose Mary? [*Sits Right of table.*]

ABIE. She went to fix the baby's milk.

MRS. COHEN. Oh, how I love babies!

ABIE. Yes, I've been a proud father just a month today.

COHEN. [*Back from foyer, hanging up things.*] Don' the time fly? And you can do so much in a little while!

MRS. COHEN. Have you heard from your father yet?

ABIE. [*Crosses to* MRS. COHEN.] No. Not a word.

COHEN. [*Brings chair down to Left of table; sits.* ABIE *is between them.*] Ve haven't mentioned it to him at all. Hev ve, Mama?

MRS. COHEN. Not a word! But he keeps talking about children all the time.

ABIE. [*Eagerly.*] Does he really?

MRS. COHEN. Says he's goink to leave all his moneys to poor children.

COHEN. Yeh and I esked him, if the money vos goink to be left just for Jewish children, und he said—

MRS. COHEN. Yes, Abie, he said it!

ABIE. Said what?

MRS. COHEN. Go on, Isaac, tell him what he said.

COHEN. How can I tell him when always you butts in? All the time!

MRS. COHEN. I butts in?

COHEN. Yes, always you butts in, Mama! [BOTH *ad lib.*]

ABIE. Well, come, come, what did he say? [*Standing between them.*]

COHEN and MRS. COHEN. [*Together.*] Well, he said—

COHEN. [*Excited.*] Mama, we can't say it together individually!

MRS. COHEN. All right, go on tell him, I don't care.

COHEN. You said tell him in the first place.

MRS. COHEN. [*Angry.*] Well, tell, I'm shut! Shtum shoin! [*Puts hand over mouth.*]

COHEN. Well, he said, he said—now you made me forget it, see that?

MRS. COHEN. [*Laughing.*] I made him forget it! [BOTH *ad lib.*]

COHEN. Abie, vhere vas I?

ABIE. Why you were saying that my father was going to leave his money to Jewish children.

MRS. COHEN. Dots it, Abie!

COHEN. Fangst shoin vider un! Don't you know the old saying silence is fourteen carats—he said "Certainly nod! His money vas goink to be all kins of childrens."

MRS. COHEN. Yes sir, Abie! He said, "can children help it vhen dhere parents are voolish?"

COHEN. Und I said, "vell vhy nod leave id to Abie's children, they're poor?"

MRS. COHEN. He said, "I'm goink to leave my money to many childrens."

COHEN. Und I said, "vell give Rose and Abie a chance, dey might hev a lot, dey certain heven't wasted any time yet."

ABIE. Poor Dad! You know I think he is just dying to

see what a son of his son's looks like. [*Crosses up to above tree.*]

COHEN. *Shure!* Vhy nod? I'd like to see it too!

MRS. COHEN. Isaac, you ain'd got a son. How can you see vhat his son looks like?

COHEN. I said if I had vone, I'd like to see it!

MRS. COHEN. But you haven't!

[ROSE MARY *enters the room.*]

COHEN. [*Crossing to* MRS. COHEN.] Mama always you argue with me here.

MRS. COHEN. But how can you see your son—

COHEN. [*Crosses to her.*] Yeh, but vhy argue in other people's houses? Soon we'll be home. Home! [*Goes up to door Center. Back to Right.*]

ROSE MARY. [*Crosses down Left of table.*] Hello, there!

MRS. COHEN. [*Goes to her and kisses her.*] Didn't expect us so late, did you?

ROSE MARY. Awfully glad you stopped in. We're waiting up for Christmas. Hello, there. [*Crosses to* COHEN.]

COHEN. [*Comes down Right.*] I'm sorry, ve can't stay a minute.

MRS. COHEN. Isaac! [*She gives him look.*]

COHEN. [*Quickly.*] Yes, ve can!

ROSE MARY. I have something awfully good to eat.

ABIE. And it's Kosher. [*Coming down Left.*]

MRS. COHEN. Papa, we're goink to stay! [*Takes off hat, puts it on service table up Left Center.*]

COHEN. Mama say we stay! We stay!

ROSE MARY. How do you like the tree? [*They* ALL *turn, look at it.*]

COHEN. [*Not very enthusiastic.*] Fine!

ROSE MARY. Abie trimmed it all by himself. [*She is bustling about like a good little housewife.*]

COHEN. You don't say so?

ROSE MARY. Excuse me, I must see about my ham, it's in the oven. [*She exits Right.* ABIE *reacts to* MRS. COHEN.]

COHEN. [*Crosses to* ABIE, *delighted.*] Abie, did she say ham?

MRS. COHEN. [*Crosses to* COHEN.] Isaac, do you ead ham?

COHEN. Vell, Mama, I tasted it vonce. You would like id!

MRS. COHEN. Abie, ham ain'd Kosher food!

ABIE. I know it isn't! The ham is for Rose Mary and her friends. The Kosher food is for me and my friends.

COHEN. I hope Rosie ain'd god too many friends.

MRS. COHEN. Isaac!! Over there! Zits!

[COHEN *jumps and goes to Left of table.*]

ABIE. Don't you worry though, it is a large ham. I bought it myself! [*The doorbell rings.*] Excuse me.

MRS. COHEN. Sure. Vy not?

[ABIE *answers bell, going to Center door. It is* FATHER WHALEN. MRS. COHEN *sits Right of table and* COHEN *Left.*]

FATHER WHALEN. Good evening, Abie!

ABIE. [*Delighted.*] Father Whalen! Come right in! Give me your hat and coat. I was never so glad to see anyone in my life! How have you been?

FATHER WHALEN. Splendid— [*Taking off his coat at the Center door.*] And how is the good wife?

ABIE. Wonderful!!

FATHER WHALEN. And the family?

ABIE. Great! You know the Cohens, Father?

[FATHER WHALEN *comes down Center.*]

FATHER WHALEN. Why, of course. [*Taking off gloves.*]

COHEN. Shure! I know de Father! Merry Christmas!

[*Both* MR. *and* MRS. COHEN *rise.*]

FATHER WHALEN. How are you both?

MRS. COHEN. Ve heven't seen you since the vedding! Oi! Vod a battle!

FATHER WHALEN. Everything seems peaceful enough now.

[ABIE *crosses toward door Right.*]

MRS. COHEN. Yes, seems dod vay.

[FATHER WHALEN *nods for them to sit, which they do.*]

ABIE. [*Calls.*] Rose Mary! Look!

ROSE MARY. [*Entering.*] Oh, Father Whalen, I can't believe my eyes! Is it really you?

FATHER WHALEN. Your eyes are not deceiving you, Rose Mary!

MRS. COHEN. [*Smiling benignly.*] She's glad to see somebody from home!

ROSE MARY. How's Father! Have you seen him lately? Is he well? He won't even write to us.

FATHER WHALEN. To be sure he's well. Fit as a fiddle!

ROSE MARY. Did he send his love?

FATHER WHALEN. No dear, not by me. [*She looks disappointed.*] But I think he would have liked to. [ROSE MARY *turns away, hides her face.*] There—there—Rose Mary! [*He motions to* ABIE *to go to her.*]

ABIE. [*Seeing that* ROSE MARY *is sad, taking her in his arms.*] Don't you care, dear! We should worry about your old father!

ROSE MARY. But I do care! He's my father!

MRS. COHEN. Vell, dod ain'd your fault!

[COHEN *shows his disgust at this remark. Bangs hand on table.* MRS. COHEN *turns to him.* COHEN *points to* FATHER WHALEN *and bangs hand on table again.* MRS. COHEN *turns back to* COHEN *and bangs table.* COHEN *is squelched.*]

ROSE MARY. [*Crosses to* MRS. COHEN *smiling, puts arm on her shoulder.*] Father Whalen come with me, I want to show you something. [*She is very sweet about this, takes* FATHER WHALEN'S *hand and leads him to door Left.*] You've never seen anything so cunning in your life!

COHEN. Oi! Such a sveetness! If I vos the papa of a sveetness like dod, I vouldn't speak to anybody!

FATHER WHALEN. Lead me to it! I'm crazy about babies! [ROSE MARY *leads the way into the room Left,* FATHER WHALEN *following.* ABIE *fixes tree.*]

ROSE MARY. Right in there, and don't make any noise. You know young babies sleep all the time!

FATHER WHALEN. [*Tiptoeing into room.*] I won't.

ROSE MARY. [*Before she exits.*] Mrs. Cohen will you look at my ham and see that it doesn't burn? [ROSE MARY *exits after* FATHER WHALEN, *closing the door.* MRS. COHEN *looks in blank amazement at* ABIE *and* COHEN.]

MRS. COHEN. Look at a ham! I never looked at a ham in my life!

COHEN. [*Amused.*] Go on, Mama, look at it! It von't bite you.

ABIE. If I knew anything about it, I'd attend to it myself!

COHEN. So vould I! [*Rising.*]

MRS. COHEN. Never mind! Zits! I'll do id— [*Crosses to*

door Right.] I'll do id, bud it's against my vill! [*With great effort she says the last and exits.* ABIE *smiles to himself.*]

COHEN. [*Crosses to* ABIE, *Right.*] I hope she don'd do anythink to spoil dod ham! I don'd trust Mama vid pork!

ABIE. [*Laughing.*] She can't do anything to hurt it!

COHEN. Vell, I'd feel safer vatching her! I'm nod goink to take any chances. She's liable to make a fish out of it. [*Exits Right.* ABIE *laughs.*]

ROSE MARY. [*Enters, followed by* FATHER WHALEN, *who closes the door.*] Abie, did she go?

ABIE. Right in where the ham is. [*Exits Right.*]

FATHER WHALEN. Where is everybody?

ROSE MARY. They're all in with the ham. Will you excuse me a second till I see if everything is all right? You know I'm chief cook and bottle washer now.

FATHER WHALEN. To be sure I will. Go right ahead! I understand! [ROSE MARY *starts to go.*] And Rose Mary— [*Goes to her.*] I have a little Christmas present for you.

ROSE MARY. Oh, what is it?

FATHER WHALEN. I'll tell you later. Go in the kitchen until I call you.

[*As soon as* ROSE MARY *exits Right,* FATHER WHALEN *goes to Center door. Opens same, beckons, walks down*

Center. A second later PATRICK *enters. He has Christ-mas toys wrapped in paper. Everything for a girl.*]

PATRICK. [*Puts package back of table.*] I wondered where you had gotten to!

FATHER WHALEN. They have company.

PATRICK. They have?

FATHER WHALEN. [*Pause.*] The Cohens! [PATRICK *who is taking off coat, makes motion as if to put it on again.*] You remember them?

PATRICK. I'd like to forget them! [*Puts coat on again, see tree, hangs coat on tree in hall.*]

FATHER WHALEN. So you've been shopping, eh?

PATRICK. Yes, I saw a little store down the street and thought I'd get a few things for my grand-daughter. [*Crosses to back of table.*]

FATHER WHALEN. Suppose it isn't that kind of a baby?

PATRICK. What—they have a boy?

FATHER WHALEN. I said, suppose!

PATRICK. A boy would have to have the name of Levy tacked on to him forever. That would be terrible!

FATHER WHALEN. [*Crosses to* PATRICK.] Well, Levy isn't a bad name.

PATRICK. Huh!

[ABIE *enters, stands very quietly. They do not see him.*]

FATHER WHALEN. If it's good enough for Rose Mary; it ought to be good enough for her baby.

PATRICK. That's the trouble! It isn't good enough for Rose Mary! Why, she is a direct descendant of the Kings of Ireland!

FATHER WHALEN. Well, Abie might be a direct descendant of the Kings of Jerusalem!

ABIE. No! Just plain Jew. But I love Rose Mary, Mr. Murphy, more than you do!

PATRICK. Oh you do, do you?

ABIE. Yes, for I wouldn't do anything in the world to cause her the tiniest bit of unhappiness. Can you say as much?

PATRICK. Listen to him! [*Turns away Left, to sideboard, looks at decanter.*]

FATHER WHALEN. The lad is right, Patrick. [*Crosses to* ABIE.] Abie, will you do something for me?

ABIE. Anything, Father!

FATHER WHALEN. Keep everybody in the kitchen as long as you can, will you?

ABIE. Don't you want Rose Mary?

FATHER WHALEN. Not yet, laddie! I'll call you! [*The doorbell rings.*] I'll answer the door! You keep them in there!

ABIE. All right! I suppose you know what you are doing, Father!

FATHER WHALEN. I do, lad, trust me!

[*As* ABIE *exits.* FATHER WHALEN *turns to see* PATRICK *looking into a whiskey decanter on sideboard. He smiles and goes to Center door, opening same. It is the* RABBI.]

RABBI. Well, well, if it isn't my old friend, John Whalen!

FATHER WHALEN. Jacob Samuels, how are you?

[*The* RABBI *enters, takes off hat and coat.* PATRICK *is sore at the interruption.*]

PATRICK. Huh! The Jew parson!

FATHER WHALEN. [*Down Center.*] Come in!

RABBI. Where are the young folks? [*Comes down Center.*]

FATHER WHALEN. [*In soft tone; pointing to kitchen.*] In there.

[RABBI *starts to go.* FATHER WHALEN *touches him on shoulder, and points to* PATRICK.]

RABBI. [*Looks at* PATRICK.] Is that Mr. Murphy?

PATRICK. [*Looking at him as though he would like to fight.*] It is that!

RABBI. You came all the way from California to spend your Christmas with Rosíe?

PATRICK. I did not. I didn't come to see Rose Mary! 'Tis the child I came to see and if it looks Irish, it gets all my money. [*Crosses to Center.* RABBI *and* FATHER WHALEN *smile at each other. Turning to* FATHER WHALEN.] Father Whalen, I'll be right back. I couldn't carry everything up the stairs at once. [*He turns and exits Center.*]

FATHER WHALEN. His bark is far worse than his bite. He's dying to see his daughter.

[BOTH *sit at table*—RABBI *Left*—FATHER WHALEN *Right*.]

RABBI. Of course he is. So is Solomon just as anxious to see his son.

FATHER WHALEN. The young folks have stuck it out. They deserve to be forgiven.

RABBI. 'Tis the young folks who should do the forgiving. Their only crime is loving not wisely but well.

FATHER WHALEN. Abie's a fine boy!

RABBI. [*Not to be outdone.*] And Rosie's a fine girl!

FATHER WHALEN. Indeed she is!

RABBI. Father, did you show Patrick the— [*Pointing to bedroom.*]

FATHER WHALEN. No, not yet. I knew he was anxious so I thought a little punishment would be good for him. The stubborn old Mick! [*They laugh.*] Patrick is sure it's a girl.

RABBI. And Solomon is just as sure it's a boy. I must take a peek myself! [*Goes to Left door, and looks out. Motions for* FATHER WHALEN *to come.*] Father did you ever see anything so sweet in your life?

FATHER WHALEN. Never! [*Looking over* RABBI's *shoulder.*] And I've seen a great many babies too!

[*They exit Left, tiptoeing off; closing the door. The*

door Center opens cautiously, and SOLOMON *sticks his head in the door. He has overcoat, hat and earmuffs on; looks in; removes coat and hat, looks in door again, then removes earmuffs, hangs them up; then enters with pillow sham containing Teddy Bear, horse, engine, drum and sticks; goes to back of table. Crosses to Right, listens, then sits on chair up Right of tree; takes out toys, places them on the floor: takes out horse, whose tail is off. He looks it over, finally finding where tail belongs and puts it on. As he puts engine on floor* PATRICK *enters with phonograph.* PATRICK *puts phonograph Left of tree, then goes to package back of table, and begins to open it,* SOLO- MON *puts drum down and* PATRICK *hears it. He looks toward door Right, then they* BOTH *spy each other.* SOLO- MON *and* PATRICK *turn, face each other,* BOTH *come Cen- ter, then sniff—turn away two steps and look at each other; then* SOLOMON *gets Teddy Bear and places it un- der the tree—*PATRICK *pushes Teddy Bear over to make room for his doll—triumphant attitude.* PATRICK *gets dolls placed under tree—same business as* SOLOMON, SOLOMON *gets horse and places Teddy Bear on it—same business.* PATRICK *unwraps go-cart, places doll in it, same business.* SOLOMON *gets engine, runs it on table several times.* PATRICK *gets phonograph, starts it—it has a record, an Irish Jig—places it under tree—dances a few steps.* SOLOMON *gets toy drum, beats it, trying to drown out jig.* PATRICK *gets toy horn, faces* SOLOMON, *blowing it.* RABBI *enters from Left followed by* FATHER WHALEN.]

RABBI. Here, here!

FATHER WHALEN. Glory be to God!

RABBI. What is this? Your second childhood? [PATRICK *and* SOLOMON *both look foolish.* PATRICK *turns off phonograph.*]

PATRICK. I wanted to see that everything worked right for my grand-daughter. [*Crosses to front of table.*]

SOLOMON. [*Rising, laughing sarcastically.*] Listen to him, he thinks it's a girl!

PATRICK. [*Glowering at him.*] Do you know what it is?

SOLOMON. No! But I know it isn't a girl!

FATHER WHALEN. Come on, Patrick, be reasonable!

SOLOMON. Oi! Oi! Such a name! Patrick! Patrick Murphy!

PATRICK. Patrick's a grand old name! It speaks for itself!

SOLOMON. Vell, ven you call Solomon, you don'd have to use your imagination.

[*All this time* FATHER WHALEN *and* RABBI *are standing back; trying to get a chance to stop them.*]

RABBI. Solomon! Solomon! [*Down to* SOLOMON.]

FATHER WHALEN. [*Down to* PATRICK.] Patrick!

SOLOMON. Oi! Dod I should live to see my son married to a Murphy!

PATRICK. Well, you may not know it, but your time has almost come!

RABBI. Come, come, this will never do! If you are going

to fight like this, it would have been better to have stayed away!

PATRICK. What? Me stay away from my grand-daughter on Christmas?

SOLOMON. She would be better, if she didn't have a grandpapa!?

PATRICK. And are you speaking for yourself?

SOLOMON. I heven't a grand-daughter!

FATHER WHALEN. Well, if you had one, I don't think she'd own you!

PATRICK. And that's no lie! [*Turning away.*]

FATHER WHALEN. Or you either, Patrick!

PATRICK. [*Surprised.*] What's the idea?

FATHER WHALEN. She'd be ashamed of the fighting. You know, Patrick, the Irish are a great people!

PATRICK. Don't I know it! [*Throwing out his chest.*]

SOLOMON. Huh! Say some more funny things!

FATHER WHALEN. And the Jews are a wonderful people!

PATRICK. That's the best joke tonight!

FATHER WHALEN. Now if the Jews and the Irish would only stop fighting, and get together, they'd own a corner of the world!

RABBI. You're right, Father, and I think they ought to start getting together right here!

PATRICK. [*Starting for* SOLOMON.] That suits me, by golly, that suits me!

SOLOMON. Pas kudnack!

FATHER WHALEN. [*Stops him; crosses to* SOLOMON.] I'm an Irishman, and I never saw a finer lad in my life than Abraham Levy!

RABBI. [*Crosses to* PATRICK.] I'm a Jew, and I never saw a finer girl in the world than Rosie!!

PATRICK. Her name isn't Rosie! It's Rose Mary!

RABBI. Very well, Rose Mary, if that pleases you better!

SOLOMON. The Rose Mary's don'd please me better! It's Rosie!

PATRICK. Whose daughter is she?

SOLOMON. She ain'd your daughter any more. You disowned her, you said so. Ain'd you?

RABBI. Here, here, neither of you should say anything! Both of you ought to be ashamed. Instead of making the best of a bad situation, you make it worse!

FATHER WHALEN. 'Tis the truth he's speaking, Patrick! [*Walks up.*]

RABBI. Now Abie and Rosie—

PATRICK. Rose Mary!
SOLOMON. Rosie! } [*Spoken together.*]

RABBI. Very well, Abie and his wife have been very happy here. For one year—neither one of you have given a cent toward helping them. And some of the times have been pretty hard. Abie only makes a small salary and Rosie has had to do all the work, even do her own washing.

SOLOMON. Vell, dod's a good pizzness for the Irish!

[*Pause.* RABBI *and* FATHER WHALEN *go up Center.* PATRICK *starts for* SOLOMON, *but* FATHER WHALEN *motions him back.*]

PATRICK. Well, that's better than peddling shoestrings!

SOLOMON. They named vonce a song "The Irish Washerwoman."

PATRICK. I could say something insulting, but I won't, you funny wizened-up-old Shylock! [*Turns away.*]

SOLOMON. Did you give them any money yourself this year? No! You stingy old A.P.A. [*Walks toward Center.*]

PATRICK. [*Starting after* SOLOMON.] Don't call me an A.P.A. I belong to the Ancient Order of Hibernians— and believe me, that ain't no A.P.A. hangout!

[FATHER WHALEN *stops him.* RABBI *goes to* SOLOMON.]

RABBI. Solomon, why do you call him an A.P.A.?

SOLOMON. I don't know. It makes him mad. [*To* FATHER WHALEN.] I never knew there vos any difference between them.

PATRICK. My God! Will you listen to the dumb thing. Any difference between them? And I live to hear such a thing!

SOLOMON. Vell, nod being Irish myself, I should know the difference. Bud—I'm glad I insulted you. I'll say it again. [RABBI *and* FATHER WHALEN *go up a few steps.*]

PATRICK. [*Going toward him threateningly.*] If you say it once more, it will be the last thing you say in this world! Now speak up, or forever hold your peace!! [*By this time he is standing over* SOLOMON.]

SOLOMON. [*Smiling up at him.*] Vell, if I say id, I vill forever hold my peace!

PATRICK. You bet you will! [*He walks away.*]

SOLOMON. I don'd have to say id!

PATRICK. [*Satisfied that he has won the battle.*] You're wise!

SOLOMON. I'll tink it! [*Laughs.*]

PATRICK. [*Spinning around immediately to him.*] Oh, you'll tink it, will you? [*Raising his fist.*]

SOLOMON. [*Blandly.*] Vell, I'm not tinking it now!

PATRICK. [*Walking away again.*] It's a good thing!

SOLOMON. Bud I have an active mind! [PATRICK *immediately turns to him again.*] I can tink of the weather— [*Snapping his fingers.*] Like dod!

PATRICK. In a few minutes, you're going to go where the weather is so hot a thermometer can't register it!

SOLOMON. Dod is good! I'll keep it dod vay for your arrival!

FATHER WHALEN. [*Center.*] Now, aren't you two ashamed of yourselves?

RABBI. Grown men! Fathers!

FATHER WHALEN. Grandfathers!

PATRICK. If you will only let me see my grand-daughter, I'll go!

SOLOMON. I vont to see Abie's first born!

RABBI. I'll bring the baby to you. [*Exits Left.*]

PATRICK. [*Right of table.*] My grand-daughter!

SOLOMON. If it's a girl, you can hev it, I don'd vant it!

FATHER WHALEN. [*Up right.*] Oh, yes you will, Mr. Levy!

PATRICK. If it's a girl she gets all my money!

SOLOMON. If she's a boy, she gets all mine!

RABBI. [*Enters.*] Father Whalen! Will you take little Patrick Joseph.

PATRICK. Patrick Joseph! A boy named for me?

FATHER WHALEN. Yes. [FATHER WHALEN *exits Left.* PATRICK *follows smiling, a few steps then faces front.*]

PATRICK. [*Gloating over the name.*] Patrick Joseph Murphy—Levy. *Oh!!!* I won't say the rest! [*Crosses front of table.*] It ought to be the happiest day of your life to think you're lucky enough! [*Places chair Right of table, and sits facing off Left*]

SOLOMON. Tut, tut—I thought you wouldn't hev a boy!

PATRICK. This is different. 'Tis named for me! [*Slams chair down in rage.*]

SOLOMON. Dod's enough! Patrick Joseph! Ph! To tink I should live to have that name in my family! [PATRICK *sits—his back to* SOLOMON.] To think my Abie's first born should be called Patrick Joseph!

PATRICK. I'm going to call my grandson Pat, for short!

SOLOMON. [*Looks daggers at* PATRICK. *Picks up chair, places it back to back to* PATRICK'S *with a bang, and sits facing off Right.*] I won't call him Patrick. I'll call him Mr. Levy!

PATRICK. That's the trouble with your race; they won't give in; acknowledge when they're beaten!

SOLOMON. Give in, is it? That's the trouble with the Irish! Dod's the reason it took you so long to get free!

PATRICK. Well, at least we've always had a country— that's more than you can say!

SOLOMON. Ve god a country, too! Jerusalem is free! Ve god it back!

PATRICK. Now that you got it, what are you going to do with it?

SOLOMON. Ve really don'd need it! Ve own all the other peoples!

PATRICK. Well, you don't own Ireland, thank God!!

SOLOMON. No, maybe dod's vot's the matter wid it! [PATRICK *rises and starts after him.* SOLOMON *holds chair up to defend himself.*]

PATRICK. I won't stand it, I won't—I'll break every bone — [*Ad lib.*]

FATHER WHALEN. [*Enters with baby, he sees the two fighting.*] Patrick! [PATRICK *turns and sees* FATHER WHALEN *with the baby which he brings to* PATRICK. PATRICK *takes the baby.*] Look out for its head.

PATRICK. [*Takes baby and crosses to chair Left of table with the greatest of care. While* SOLOMON *sorrowfully looks on.*] Hello, Pat! [*Sits.*]

SOLOMON. Oi, Pat! [*Cries, sits Right.*]

RABBI. [*Enters with other baby. He goes to* SOLOMON *while* FATHER WHALEN *closes door, and comes to Right of table.* RABBI *stands beside* SOLOMON.] Solomon!

SOLOMON. [*His head bowed, gradually raises his head, sighing.*] Ah, what's the use? [*He sees baby, looks at* PATRICK, *sees other baby, then rises delighted.*] Twinses?

RABBI. Yes.

PATRICK. Glory be to God!

SOLOMON. [*Stands up.*] My Abie is a smart boy; you see —he wouldn't forget his old papa. Doctor Samuels, is this one named after my papa?

RABBI. No, Solomon, it couldn't be. It's a girl!

SOLOMON. [*His expression changes.*] Take it back—I don't vant it!

RABBI. Oh, yes you do—it's a wonderful baby. Come, Solomon, look at her!

SOLOMON. I wouldn't do it.

RABBI. Poor little Rebecca—

SOLOMON. [*His heart softens.*] Rebecca—that's a fine name. Give me a look. [*He takes baby quickly from* RABBI.]

RABBI. Look out, Solomon, look out for its head.

SOLOMON. Dot's all right, I was a baby vonce. [*He goes to chair Right of table, sits.*]

PATRICK. Father Whalen. [*Motions for him, whispers.* FATHER WHALEN *goes to him.*] Are you sure this is the boy?

FATHER WHALEN. Certainly, it has the pink ribbon.

PATRICK. I haven't much confidence in ribbon.

SOLOMON. [*Motions for* RABBI.] Doctor Samuels, sometimes they get twinses mixed.

RABBI. They haven't been mixed, Solomon. You have little Rebecca!

SOLOMON. [*Playing with baby.*] Yeh! Coochy coo! [*Takes rattle from pocket, and shakes it.*]

PATRICK. [*Takes chicken balloon from his pocket and blowing it up, stands it on table. Holds baby to see.*] Look, Pat!

[RABBI *and* FATHER WHALEN *laugh and exeunt Right.*]

SOLOMON. Rebecca, look! [*After wind is out of chicken.*] Look for nothing.

PATRICK. [*Who is beginning to get lost in the interest of the baby.*] Shure, I have to give Abie credit—the boy here is the dead image of him!

SOLOMON. [*Delighted.*] No, is it?

PATRICK. Look! [BOTH *rise.* SOLOMON *goes a bit closer and looks at the baby.*]

SOLOMON. He is, isn't he?

PATRICK. Didn't I tell you?

SOLOMON. Und the girl is just like Rosie! She's beautiful! Give a look!

[*Each is looking at the baby in the other man's arms.*]

PATRICK. She looks just like my little Rose Mary! It takes me back to the time I first held her in my arms—her mother didn't live!

SOLOMON. [*Softly.*] Abie's didn't too!

PATRICK. I wonder if you'd mind if I held little Rebecca in me arms for awhile!

SOLOMON. Certainly nod! Give me little Patrick! [*They look for some place to put the babies to exchange. Finally* PATRICK *puts his on table, and takes baby from* SOLOMON.] Look out for the cup.

PATRICK. What???

SOLOMON. Excuse me, please, look out for its head!

PATRICK. Ah, talk United States! Ah shure, I feel more natural with a girl! Guess I'm more used to it!

SOLOMON. [*Puzzled at how to pick up the baby, picks it up.*] Me too! I feel more natural vid a boy! Patrickal! [*They both sing lullabies,* SOLOMON *singing "Oyitzki Iz*

Gegangen, etc." PATRICK *singing "Too-ra-loo-ra-loo-ra."*]

PATRICK. She ought to be called Rose Mary.

SOLOMON. Yes, maybe some day she could marry a good Irishman like yourself, and keep it all alike, yes?

PATRICK. You know, Sol.

SOLOMON. Yes, Pat?

PATRICK. That boy should be named for you. Solomon Levy.

SOLOMON. Solomon. It does sound better!

PATRICK. Let's change the names!

SOLOMON. Maybe Abie and Rosie vont let us!

[ROSE MARY *enters Right followed by* ABIE. *They go over to their parents and look down over their shoulders; the men do not see them.*]

PATRICK. To be sure, they'll let us!

SOLOMON. Maybe we could apologize and esk them to fergive us.

PATRICK. Well, if I can feel ashamed of myself, and I am—God knows you ought to be!

SOLOMON. [*Resents the insult, then smiles.*] I feel like ten cents worth of liverwurst!

[ROSE MARY *and* ABIE *run to their fathers,* ROSE MARY *kisses* PATRICK *and* ABIE *puts his arm around* SOLOMON.]

ROSE MARY. Daddy!

ABIE. Oh, Dad!

SOLOMON. It's all right!

[MRS. COHEN *enters Right followed by* COHEN *carrying four plates.* RABBI *and* FATHER WHALEN *also enter Right.*]

MRS. COHEN. Merry Christmas! [*She is carrying the ham.*]

SOLOMON. Mrs. Cohen, vod is dod you're carrying?

MRS.COHEN. It's a baked ham! [*She crosses and puts it on table, followed by* COHEN *with plates.*]

[SOLOMON'S *smile disappears. The Christmas bells start to ring out.*]

SOLOMON. Vod iss it? A fire?

PATRICK. A fire! 'Tis Christmas! Merry Christmas, Sol!

SOLOMON. Goot Yonteff, Patrick!

CURTAIN
END OF PLAY

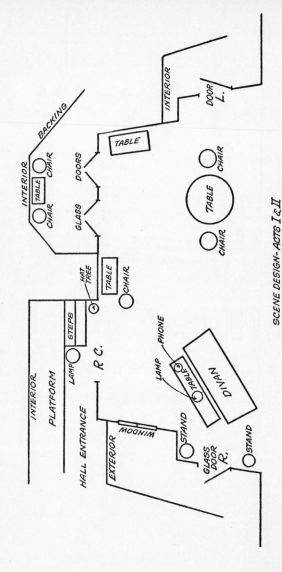

SCENE DESIGN—ACTS I & II
"ABIE'S IRISH ROSE"

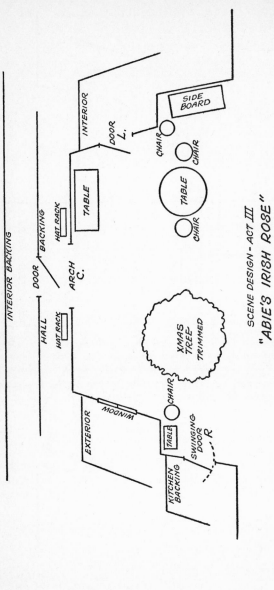

SCENE DESIGN - ACT III
"ABIE'S IRISH ROSE"